Sugar and Dirt

memoirs of a tortoise

Fernando Prol

Sugar and Dirt: Memoirs of a Tortoise

Published by Wheatmark®
1760 East River Road, Suite 145, Tucson, Arizona 85718 U.S.A.

www.wheatmark.com

ISBN: 978-1-62787-163-1 (paperback)
ISBN: 978-1-62787-164-8 (ebook)
LCCN: 2014911688

Author photo by Scott Leska

Cover design by Lori Leavitt of Wheatmark

Para mi madre y padre, y mi hermano;
And for Laura and Nick.

Contents

Editor's Introduction

AT THE AGE OF SIXTY, just a few weeks following his retirement from a forty-year career as an employee for several municipalities' public works and engineering departments, F.P. Romero's life came to a sad and sudden end due to a ruptured brain aneurism. Unfortunately, to my way of thinking anyway, following F.P.'s death there was an unseemly and odd debate among the doctors—and several family members—about the primary source of F.P.'s aneurism. I was informed that according to one of the doctors in question, the aneurism may have been the direct result of some kind of head trauma F.P. had suffered many years earlier. I was also told that several of the other doctors strongly disagreed with that opinion, stating in their findings that the aneurism most likely occurred due to a more recent cause. Why the source of the aneurism became such a point of contention I never understood until some time later when I learned that for certain folks F.P.'s past was a very prickly subject.

The day of his funeral in Snowflake, Arizona, my

stepsister Kahmeh, F.P.'s widow, spoke to me with great passion about F.P.'s unfinished autobiographical work, *Sugar and Dirt*, which she strongly felt was far enough along in its telling of F.P.'s unique story to be very much worth publishing. She asked that I, a long-time editor for a now-defunct small-town newspaper (with a circulation of three thousand, give or take) in our home state of Kansas, serve as the book's editor. In her delicately tenacious Japanese way, my wonderful stepsister has always been a very persuasive person, and I could not turn her down.

Over the next several months, I communicated with Kahmeh via the telephone or e-mails on numerous occasions regarding what she knew of F.P.'s overall intent and plan for the book, especially in reference to the three different types of texts included in F.P.'s manuscript, each type of text collated in a separate binder according to its category. The distinct texts included straightforward, first-person narratives in chapter form (Chapters 1–8 and 13); other narratives that fell outside of the chapters' more linear chronology and that F.P. titled as "Lost and Found"; and poems that F.P. had called "parallel verses." (Kahmeh informed me that F.P. did not like to refer to these verses as poems as he felt that considering himself a poet was "pretentious nonsense.") The binder with the narrative chapters also included an author's postscript and a letter from F.P. to his father.

Kahmeh knew that F.P. intended to include all three

types of texts in the book but did not know the order in which he wished to present them. So, other than making some mostly minor grammar and syntax revisions, my primary editorial task was to assemble the different texts in an order I felt was the most logical and in conformance with what I believe was F.P.'s intent—of course, with Kahmeh's express approval. According to Kahmeh, F.P. wrote the "Lost and Found" narratives and the "parallel verses" so that they would foreshadow or expand on events, places, and persons related in upcoming or previous chapters. I have done my best to place them among the chapters in a fashion that I hope properly reflects F.P.'s intent.

On a more personal note: I never got to know F.P. very well, as we only chatted casually at the infrequent family functions held throughout the years. However, I do know Kahmeh well enough to be certain that she would not have stuck with F.P. through more than thirty years of marriage had he not been an upstanding man, a good husband, and a loving father to their daughter, Yuki. Kahmeh always expressed her great pride in F.P. and the professional success he attained, rising from a laborer position to higher management, even though he never obtained a college degree.

Even though my acquaintance with F.P. was not extensive, I was always impressed with his manner, his personal demeanor. He conveyed a quiet, implicit self-assurance and nobility that with anyone else may have come across as haughtiness or condescension. The best

way I can describe it is he had something of an aristocratic bearing about him. It was only later, as I edited
his book, that I learned the probable source of his distinctive conduct.

—Ernest Scott-Thomas
Terrapin Flats, Kansas, USA

Sugar and Dirt

memoirs of a tortoise

"God writes straight with crooked lines."

— Spanish proverb

"To live is to change, and if you have lived long, you have changed often."

—John Henry Newman

"Tell all the Truth but tell it slant—Success in Circuit lies"

—Emily Dickinson

Caveat Lector
(In Lieu of a Preface)

THIS BOOK IS A PRODUCT of my imagination, abetted by my memory—or is it the other way around? Either way, the book is chock-full of autobiographical truths. Due to the mostly unchaperoned commingling of imagination and memory as touched upon above, and to ensure that absolutely no offense is given to any living or deceased person, I have gently persuaded some of the autobiographical truths to arrive on our stage bearing somewhat altered appearances. This, I believe they have done in a most laudable—and sometimes surprising—fashion. In fact, some of the truths that have turned up have been totally unrecognizable to me—either that, or I simply do not recall having ever been introduced to them. I should note that the truths have beseeched me, as their sole counsel and agent in this matter, to unequivocally affirm and testify to the reliability and integrity of their trueness. That, I hereby do, but with extreme and true reluctance.

F.P.R.

An Overture of Sorts

A picaresque trek will here be mapped;
Both delight and despair will be felt;
Shell-hard armor will need to be strapped;
And some marked cards will surely be dealt.

Our tortoise-like hero will awaken,
Awfully fervent to join the race!
High-wire risks by our Achilles will be taken,
E'er endangering his carapace.

Sugar and dirt will certainly be blended,
To be dutifully and often tasted;
The garden of grief will be achingly tended;
The seeds of wrath shall not be wasted.

Our champion will scrap with manifold sorrows;
And he shall bathe in the bountiful bliss;
He will wink at all threatening tomorrows;
Always enduring … and thus becoming this.

part one

El Niño—Apollo

El Llanero Solitario

The Lone Ranger (El Llanero Solitario), dubbed in Spanish, was of one of our favorite television shows in Cuba. It's funny the things one gets to thinking about sometimes; the other day I was trying to remember whether the Lone Ranger called his horse Seelver or Plata on Cuban television. I just don't remember. However, I do remember my brother, Jorge, and I giggling every time we heard Tonto's name, because it means "stupid" in Spanish. Oh, the silly things we remember.

Chapter 1

THE FOLLOWING PAGES CONTAIN THE story of my youth, which I think was peculiar but certainly not extraordinary, except possibly for its seemingly senseless jumbling of random joys, broken innocence, and my own unbridled foolishness. Only in that particular sense would I venture to say that it was sort of extraordinary. To tell the truth, I just don't know what to make of it sometimes.

* * * *

I was born in Havana, Cuba, on April 14, 1954. Incidentally, April 14 is not a very propitious date, as that is the same date on which Lincoln was shot and the Titanic struck the iceberg. I truly hope no one has ever thought of me as a calamity.

Both of my parents were full-blooded Spaniards, although my mother was born in Cuba. So, I guess that makes me a full-blooded Spaniard who was born in Cuba and has lived in the United States for fifty-three of my sixty years. My father and mother's families both originated in Galicia, in northwestern Spain. My father was very proud of being a Gallego; I don't remember my mother ever mentioning her Gallego lineage. Many Gallegos immigrated to Cuba, as that was their land of opportunity during the 1920s and '30s. My understanding is that Fidel Castro's parents were Gallegos.

I know that the term is bandied about quite indiscriminately nowadays, but my father was a true Renaissance man; he was an attorney, a professor of law and languages, a primary owner of a bank, a restaurateur, and a very prosperous businessman, owning Esso gas stations throughout Cuba. Not bad for a poor farm boy from the mountains of Galicia who arrived in Cuba nearly penniless. And he loved to design houses; in fact, he designed our house in Cuba, which was designed in the Frank Lloyd Wright style.

My mother, who passed away when I was ten years old, was also a remarkable person. She was an attorney for the Cuban public transit system and one of the first women to serve on the Cuban Supreme Court. Later, in the United States, she and my father both earned master's degrees in education.

I suppose my honest and hardworking parents would have been considered members of the bloodsucking wealthy elite so despised by the Castro regime, which came to power in 1959. Prior to losing everything during Castro's revolution, we owned a lovely home in one of Havana's most affluent neighborhoods and belonged to the prestigious Havana Yacht Club. Jorge and I each had a nanny to take care of us, and we attended one of the finest parochial schools in Cuba. I have always had a special affection for Vladimir Nabokov's autobiographi-

cal *Speak, Memory*, since I think we shared similar child-
hoods and both lost magic kingdoms when we lost our
homelands. He just got to enjoy his a little longer.

*   *   *   *

Not long after Castro took over, the greater part of
our house, which no longer belonged to us, was seques-
tered by a couple dozen of Castro's soldiers. Of course,
during this time my parents never divulged to Jorge and
me their true feelings about the Castro revolution, as it
would have been extremely risky for them to do so. So,
as far as I was concerned, our house had been taken over
by a bunch of green-uniformed, mostly bearded heroes
with very cool guns.

And after months of occupying our house, one day
they were all gone. A week or so later, I found out why.
One of my most indelible memories is that of waking
up on the day after my seventh birthday to the sound of
what I thought were fireworks. Being the spoiled tyke
that I was, I believed it was a belated fireworks display
for which I had specifically asked my parents for my
birthday. In actuality, what I heard was the distant explo-
sions of bombs being dropped by B-26s on Cuban air-
fields during the onset of what came to be known as the
Bay of Pigs invasion, organized and funded by the "evil"
Americans. The bombing and the sound of heavy artillery fire continued off and on for several days. When the
triumphant soldiers whom I worshipped returned to our
house a few weeks later, they presented me with several
nifty empty artillery shells used to defeat the invaders. I
was ecstatic.

* * * *

At this time my father, who was still a Spanish citizen, sought the assistance of the Spanish embassy in Havana and succeeded in obtaining the Castro regime's permission for us to leave Cuba. Unfortunately, the permission to leave applied only to my father's immediate family; other family members such as my mother's parents and sister would have to remain. However, before it was time for us to leave, both my father and my cousin Arturo were arrested.

Arturo was in his twenties and was like a son to my father and like a marvelous older brother to Jorge and me. A couple of years back my father had arranged for him to leave Spain and come to Cuba to manage the gas stations. Arturo lived with us and brought great joy and humor to our home. He was witty and spirited, exuding confidence and vigor—an irrepressible, unfettered Gallego; but, unfortunately, one with more mettle than prudence.

Apparently Arturo had become involved with a counterrevolutionary group that was waging guerrilla warfare against the Castro regime, blowing up military facilities, power plants, and other government infrastructure, and wreaking as much havoc as possible. Unknown to my father—as far as I know, anyway—Arturo and his coconspirators were using the Esso gas stations' work bays to conceal the vehicles they used in their attacks. Sadly, Arturo was arrested and thrown into one of Che Guevara's horrific prisons.

This was a terrible time for anti-Castro Cubans, including those who, like my parents, also opposed Batista, the repressive caudillo deposed by Castro. My parents, like countless others, had yearned for a democratic, more autonomous Cuba. But Castro had triumphed and numerous Cubans were imprisoned, and many were summarily executed following farcical Stalinist-type show trials that were televised to intimidate those who opposed the new tyrant. And, undoubtedly, Castro did a masterful job of duping the world's press into thinking he was a true and tolerant democrat who would eventually allow free elections, freedom of speech and a free press. The Cuban people are still waiting.

Arturo was imprisoned until 1968, at which time he was allowed to return to Spain. We visited him there during the summer of that year, and he, looking skinny, haggard, and very much aged, recounted many harrowing stories about the horrendous treatment that he and others had received at the hands of Che's sadistic henchmen.

* * * *

My father was of course devastated by Arturo's arrest, for he loved him dearly. And I have always wondered just how much he actually knew of what Arturo was up to. From what I understand, following his own arrest soon after Arturo's, he spent a few days being interrogated by Che's men but was released soon after. Again, I think his connections with the Spanish Embassy must have helped to free him.

Looking back at this period in my life, the resilience

or, more frankly, the obliviousness of children such as Jorge and myself greatly intrigues me. While all of this disruption and chaos was transpiring around us, we ignored everything except our own pleasures and appetites. It wasn't that we were excessively selfish or self-centered children; we were just kids surviving emotionally as best we could. The only thing that really bothered us during this time was when that megalomaniacal Castro would preempt our favorite television shows so he could give one of his interminable, haranguing speeches.

On the other hand, my parents' lives were shattered, as Castro's regime had illicitly confiscated everything my parents owned: every business, every parcel of property, every car, every piece of furniture, and every single centavo that was rightfully and honestly theirs, earned through hard work and perseverance. When we finally left Cuba we were allowed to leave with five American dollars and the clothes on our backs. I cannot begin to comprehend the pain, the apprehension, and the anguish that my parents must have felt as they lost everything and were forced to leave all that they cherished behind. I know that it was especially difficult for my mother as she was leaving all of her family behind. And I am fairly certain that at that time my parents already knew about my mother's cancer.

* * * *

I do not know the exact date, but sometime in mid-July 1961, we boarded a prop plane at the Aeropuerto José

Martí in Havana and flew away from our beloved emerald, dragon-shaped isle of Cuba, compelled to part with our home and our culture. Ironically, on that day the Soviet Air Force was putting on some kind of acrobatic air show over the airport—the interloper trying to impress the locals, I guess.

From what I've been told, we had not obtained the Cuban government's permission to fly to the United States. So, we flew to Merida, Mexico, and not long after to Tegucigalpa, Honduras, where friends of my parents lodged us for a few weeks and loaned them the money to enable us to fly to the United States.

I clearly recall that while we were in Merida, my father sat Jorge and me on the hotel room's bed and, treating us in a very adult manner, explained in detail the truth behind Castro's revolution and the politics involved in what had happened to us and Arturo. I remember feeling somewhat confused; after all, since Castro's revolution the United States had been depicted as the "evil capitalists" who might invade any day and take over our country. On the other hand, however, I always adored those blond béisbol gods, Mickey Mantle and Roger Maris, so somehow I sensed that I would undoubtedly be okay in the land of the Yankees.

My August 9

My August 9, although of crucial importance to me, pales in significance when compared to the momentous historical events that also occurred on that date. On August 9, 48 BCE Julius Caesar handily defeated his main rival for power, Pompey the Great, at the Battle of Pharsalus. The United States dropped an atomic bomb, dubbed Fat Man, on Nagasaki, Japan, on August 9, 1945. And on August 9, 1974, Richard Nixon became the first American president to resign from office. My August 9 (1961), as humble and negligible a historical date as it may be in comparison, was a day of immense consequence for the Romero family. On that day we flew out of Tegucigalpa, Honduras, and landed at Miami International Airport, USA. It is a date that I quietly celebrate every year.

Chapter 2

WE LIVED IN MIAMI FOR about a year, housed in a tiny one-bedroom duplex unit, maybe six hundred square feet in size at most. My parents slept in the bedroom, and Jorge and I camped out nightly on folding cots in the living room. I suppose the housing was provided to us by the same Cuban-refugee organization that also delivered weekly care packages filled with cans of Spam, soups, vegetables, and Kool-Aid. These same benevolent folks also drove us to a warehouse full of donated clothes where we picked out our new wardrobes.

This was a very daunting and stressful time for my parents. I remember my mother crying often and acting in an angry, peevish fashion that was very unlike her. And my father's worrying about our future was palpable, as was his great frustration with learning the English language. It wasn't as if we were experiencing a life of severe want and suffering—because we weren't. I think what wounded my parents most was the dramatic, down-spiraling transformation from their

Cuban lifestyle of comfort and familiarity to their new, bewildering, and alien reality. I believe it was extremely painful for them to awaken every day only to realize that they had lost their Eden and were now living in a strange, intimidating, and sometimes incomprehensible world. And the English language was their most pitiless foe.

I remember many evenings when all of us sat in the living room of that small house in Miami, forming a circle around a borrowed Zenith record player, listening to and repeating English phrases as vocalized by a Berlitz language-learning record. It was a long time before my parents felt comfortable with their English, and for years Jorge and I always answered the telephone at home, helping to translate conversations for our parents and to read and write much of their correspondence.

American culture also seemed intent on undermining my parents' self-respect and confidence. One sad but comic example of their immigrant pathos comes to mind. During our first Halloween night in this country my bemused father handed out cans of Spam and assorted canned vegetables from our boxes of donated food to incredulous, costumed American children because he knew nothing about this most puzzling holiday. For days he angrily wondered aloud why such a rich country's parents would send their children out begging for food.

* * * *

On the other hand, Jorge and I, more easily acclimated than our parents, were certainly not suffering or heart-broken about our plight. Our innate fortitude would just not allow that. I have always believed that Jorge and I were blessed with extremely sturdy and adaptive person-alities, always the smiling chameleons, always the desert flowers flourishing through periodic droughts. Through-out all of the challenges and tribulations that we expe-rienced then and during the coming years, Jorge and I didn't just passively float on the troubled waters, waiting for someone to come to our rescue; we swam and swam hard, sometimes in the wrong direction and sometimes against the current—especially me—but, damn it, we did swim. And so we swiftly assimilated into a culture with which both of us fell in love in our own different ways.

In our effort to learn English, television was the strongest and most engaging ally Jorge and I had. During the early 1960s, there were many memorable shows on television to which Jorge and I quickly became addicted—programs such as *The Dick Van Dyke Show, My Three Sons, Gunsmoke, The Andy Griffith Show, Leave It to Beaver,* and the classic cartoons: *The Flintstones, The Yogi Bear Show, Rocky and Bullwinkle, The Huckleberry Hound Show,* and many others. Watching all of those shows not only facilitated our becoming Americanized but, from a more practical perspective, it taught Jorge and me how to speak English.

Not that it was an immediate and painless enterprise for us. I will never forget the dreaded first day of school at Seminole Elementary, less than a month since our arrival in this country, when my father, holding each of us by the hand, led Jorge and me up to the school's main entrance and very patiently taught two very frightened little boys to say, "Mee no speek Eenglish." That was really all the English we knew when we entered that scary school. Yet, less than six months later—and, yes, after some ignominious crying in class—thanks to the many hours we had spent watching television, Jorge and I had become fairly fluent English speakers. Before long we were singing and twisting with Chubby Checker, joking with our friends, and availing ourselves of some choice curse words; one of us was even telling a cute little redhead named Margaret how much he liked her. At school we were ducking and covering under our desks during air-raid drills with the best of them, and at home, thanks to television and baseball cards, we were becoming true aficionados of American baseball. The smiling chameleons had adapted.

*　*　*　*

A few months after our arrival in the United States my mother was hospitalized for several weeks. I do not recall being told at the time the reason for her hospitalization, but later we learned that she had undergone a single mastectomy. I remember how sickly pale and weak my sweet, brave mother appeared when she returned from the hospital. And one harpy-like memory of that time by which I will always be haunted is of me cruelly back talking to her when she asked that I do some simple thing for her. In response she, shockingly out of character, screamed at me and, with a ferocity that still crushes my soul when I remember it, violently swept the toy soldiers with which I was playing off my bed. At that terrible moment I realized the overwhelming despair and suffering my angel mother was experiencing. I believe that her ingenuous and gentle disposition had not constitutionally or emotionally prepared her to cope with the juggernaut of misery and pain that life had so suddenly hurled at her. Also at that moment, as I grasped many years later, I was being fitted for the shell-hard armor I would eventually wear for the rest of my life.

* * * *

Of course, my father was also suffering, but I believe his suffering was far different than my mother's. His agony was of a more singular nature, for he was a much more durable and resolute individual than my mother. His Gallego heart was much stouter than my mother's. My father's suffering was of the type engendered not just by the deep sorrow he undoubtedly felt due to my mother's illness, but also by the agonizing loss of honor, esteem, and prominence he experienced from the sudden collapse of his personal realm in Cuba. Here was a man who was deserted by his father as a child; who tenaciously struggled his way out of a primitive mountain village in Spain; who had the pluck and temerity to emigrate to Cuba in his early twenties with hardly a centavo in his pocket; and who after years of study, sweat, and perseverance had earned his fortune and distinction. He was an indomitable and bold man.

Not long after my mother came home from the hospital, my father left us for a month or so. It was only later that we learned that he had traveled to Boston to take an immersion-type class in English. We never understood why he went all the way to Boston for this. What most shocked and saddened us about this sojourn of his was what he also did while in Boston. During those winter months—and he loathed cold weather—he earned money by washing dishes at a local hospital. To better convey the mortification and indignity that such a job must have represented for my inordinately proud father, I need to further elucidate his distinctive character and bearing.

The most succinct way to describe my father's character and manner is by using the expression *monarch in exile*. His personality and demeanor were those of the quintessential monarch in exile. There is a reasonable chance that even the most fleeting encounter with my father would have left you wondering whether you hadn't just happened upon some royal in hiding that had been unceremoniously chased out of his kingdom by rabid revolutionaries and forced to live incognito among the common folk. His bearing was that of an unapologetic philosopher king, aristocratic to the bone. His gravitas and dignitas were hard-earned and, therefore, that much more imposing. When he fixed upon you that piercing, tango-dancer's look of his, with his deep-set, black Spanish eyes, you either wilted into sweaty trepidation or swooned with abject admiration.

My monarch-in-exile father was a magnificent man.

Maryland, My Maryland

"Ain't the beer cold?" Anyone who lived in Baltimore—or Maryland for that matter—during the 1960s and '70s will likely recognize those as the words of the legendary radio and television sportscaster for the Orioles and Colts, Chuck Thompson. For decades Baltimore sports fans heard their beloved Chuck ecstatically shout his signature question whenever things were going well for the Orioles or Colts. And fans knew the beer Chuck was referring to was the unpretentious, blue-collar Natty Boh (National Bohemian), brewed right there in Baltimore and served for years at Memorial Stadium.

I miss them all so much: Chuck Thompson, Natty Boh, The Land of Pleasant Living, Brooks, Frank and Boog, Johnny U., blue crabs, skipjacks working the Chesapeake, ladies from Ballmer, Merlin calling you "Hon."

Maryland, my Maryland indeed; I will always love that state.

Oh Captain, My Captain

On November 22, 1946, a memorial to alumni who had given their lives in the two world wars was dedicated at McCullough Academy, a military school in Baltimore County, Maryland. The memorial included the Quadrangle of Honor, whose centerpiece was the Honor Stone, an eight-foot-tall marble monument inscribed with the names of McCullough's fallen heroes.

It became a tradition that when marching to John McCullough Stadium for every home football game, always on Friday afternoons, the McCullough cadet corps would stop at the Quadrangle and stand in their appointed companies along its perimeter. During this pause in their march, the highest-ranking cadet present would command the corps to attention and announce the bugler's playing of Taps in memory of McCullough's graduates who had not returned home from the wars.

Seventeen years later, to the day, I was one of the corps assembled on the perimeter of the Quadrangle of Honor. I remember standing at parade rest, my feet planted apart, my hands clasped together behind me and positioned on my lower back. As usual, our companies had first formed on the parking lot next to the school's cafeteria, from which we had marched with mournful tread to the precise, martial beat of snare drums.

During that afternoon rumors had been flying around campus like angry wasps maliciously worrying us. Since the official notice had apparently arrived very recently, the game against our archrival, Tillman School, had not been called off. Somehow, through the inexplicable means by which such news is sometimes surreptitiously delivered to each one of us, we all were aware of the tragedy.

Adding to the afternoon's pervasive solemnity, that fall day was overcast and blustery. I recall that the always dignified oaks and maples bordering the quadrangle were nearly bare, most of their leaves having fallen cold and dead; a few brave leaves nervously hung on for their dear lives like exhausted trapeze artists. The companies' guidon flags snapped angrily with each gust. Across from the quadrangle, as customary during Tillman Game Week, several effigies of uniformed Tillman players dangled out of Kyle Building's dorm windows, swinging weirdly in the wind. Bed-sheet banners screaming "Beat Tillman!" could not control themselves in the bursts of wind and found it very difficult to display their war-cry messages.

After laying a beribboned wreath at the foot of the Honor Stone, the corps' lieutenant colonel called us to attention. During the few seconds that followed, the wind momentarily subsided as if out of respect, allowing me to just make out the sound of muted weeping all around me. The colonel then declared in a voice subdued but resolutely clear, "Taps will be played in memory of McCullough's alumni who have fallen in service to their country … and the President, John F. Kennedy."

Chapter 3

MY FAMILY LEFT MIAMI IN July of 1962 because my father had accepted a teaching position in Baltimore. He had also been offered a teaching position in Lincoln, Nebraska.

From what I learned later, my father did not apply for a teaching position in the Miami area because he and my mother had decided not to stay there. Considering that at the time Miami was the place where Cuban refugees largely felt most at home, this was an atypical and intrepid decision on their part.

In 1962 the vast majority of Cubans living in Miami believed with the fervent certitude of those recently dispossessed of their homeland that they would soon be returning to their Castro-confiscated homes. They had no doubt that the Castro revolution would dissolve as quickly as snow on a Havana sidewalk.

My parents thought differently. My father in particular was intent on separating us from our compatriots. The Monarch in Exile was wise enough to grasp that the Castro regime was not going to melt away anytime in the near future, especially after the Bay of Pigs fiasco. He recognized that the soundest strategy for our family was to reconcile ourselves to the fact that we were not returning to Cuba anytime soon and that we, Jorge and I especially, would benefit most by assimilating into this country that had so benevolently welcomed us. He knew that the last thing the Miami Cubans were thinking about was assimilating, and so he wanted us away from there.

*   *   *   *

The decision to move to Baltimore was one of the most critical my parents ever made with regard to Jorge and me. It was a decision whose consequences would help to sculpt our individual characters more than any other decision they made. And I believe the decision was an acutely difficult one for my father.

The position offered to my father in Baltimore was teaching high school Spanish at McCullough Academy. The position in Lincoln, also teaching Spanish, was at the University of Nebraska. Knowing the Monarch in Exile, bless his proud Galician heart, there is little doubt in my mind that a substantial part of him greatly preferred the opportunity to teach at a prominent American university, with all of the potential for a future professorship that that entailed, than at a high school in Baltimore.

He chose McCullough, however, because the more paternal part of him (although I have no doubt that my mother played a key role in the decision) wanted to do what was best for his sons. For, as I'm sure they had learned, McCullough was considered one of the most prestigious prep schools on the East Coast.

McCullough was a military academy teaching first through twelfth grades, founded in 1873, and educating students from all over the United States and the world. As we would soon discover, it was an eight-hundred-acre world of its own, with its venerable Greek-columned and ivy-shrouded buildings, its oak and maple-cloaked campus, and its sprawling Eton-like playing fields. It was an elite school where only the sons of privilege attended and, obviously, a school that my parents could never have afforded at that time. When they learned that the children of a faculty member could attend for free, I think their decision to choose Baltimore quickly became a foregone conclusion.

I will always be grateful to my parents for not passing up the opportunity to allow Jorge and me to attend McCullough, and I know that for my father, the Monarch in Exile, it was a great sacrifice.

*   *   *   *

The first place we lived in Baltimore was a row house in Pimlico, not far from the famous racetrack of the same name. We stayed there for about a year, during which time Jorge and I began to absorb the distinctive Baltimore and Maryland culture. It wasn't long before we had switched our baseball allegiance from the Yankees to the Orioles and, of course, to the Colts in football. Football was new to us, and we were totally enamored with the sport. We were so crazy about football but still so ignorant of its finer points that I recall we actually sat down to watch the film version of *The Hunchback of Notre Dame*, thinking it was about football. Quasimodo was certainly no Knute Rockne!

From Pimlico we moved to a two-bedroom apartment atop a mom-and-pop grocery store at the intersection of Reisterstown Road and Slade Avenue, which got us closer to McCullough for our daily commutes. The couple who owned the store was very kind to us, especially as my mother's health worsened. I'll always remember running down the stairs to the store every time I got my weekly allowance so I could stock up on Hostess fruit pies, candy bars, and comic books. I also recall the weekly Saturday walks to the Pikesville Laundromat with my mother, lugging our full bags of laundry for blocks but not feeling their weight one bit since I knew that every such trip also included a visit to the Pratt Public Library across the street from the Laundromat. I knew I'd be returning home with a precious haul of books, some of which I'd be devouring like a famished man that very evening.

It was in that creaky-floored apartment that always resounded with the Reisterstown Road traffic noise that I watched on television two of the most momentous events of the 1960s. The first was the November 1963 days-long coverage of John F. Kennedy's assassination and funeral—including the shocking on-air killing of the assassin, Lee Harvey Oswald, by Jack Ruby. The second was a much more joyful and entertaining event: the earth-shaking appearance of the Beatles on *The Ed Sullivan Show* in February 1964.

The fact that two such consequential but antithetical events occurred within a few short months of each other is just another blatant example of history's brazen sense of irony. The first helped to imbue my generation with a simmering sense of disillusionment and nihilism that only grew more heated with the deaths of Martin Luther King, Jr. and Bobby Kennedy and that finally boiled over with Vietnam. Conversely, the second event infused us with the life-affirming, unshackled spirit of rock and roll that to this day continues to invigorate many of our lives. These events were, in their disparity, as black and white as their broadcasts were on our family's television.

* * * *

I spent all of fourth grade and most of fifth grade living in the Reisterstown Road apartment. As my mother's health deteriorated and it got to the point where she and my father were spending more time at the hospital than at home, my parents decided it would be best for Jorge and me to have our family live on the McCullough campus, where faculty apartments were available in the dorm buildings. Living on campus would provide Jorge and me with a safe and secure environment where all of our needs would be taken care of. The campus contained a cafeteria, an infirmary, two libraries, two basketball gyms, an indoor swimming pool, a chapel, and all of the open spaces that two athletic and rambunctious boys could desire. And on campus there were the many thoughtful and caring people who made up the extremely tightknit McCullough family.

Jorge and I attended McCullough for a total of five

years (1962–1967), during which the very bedrock of our characters and personalities was formed. During the last two and a half years of the McCullough chapter of our lives, we lived in an idyllic, tranquil, and tradition-filled environment that embodied our home, our school, our refuge, and our playground. I do not believe that I exaggerate or oversentimentalize my feelings toward McCullough when I say that the school served the symbolic role of a kind and loving stepmother to us after my mother passed away.

It is only recently that the concept of McCullough serving as our stepmother has come to mind. By coincidence, on a particular day a few months back, a day during which, for no specific reason, I had been thinking much about McCullough, I also happened to be reading a book on Abraham Lincoln. In that book I read a passage about Lincoln's great love and appreciation for his stepmother, Sarah. Sarah had married Lincoln's father not long after the death of Lincoln's mother, and she had greatly influenced Lincoln's yearning for knowledge and his overall character. As Lincoln affirmed on many occasions, everything that he became he owed to Sarah, his "angel mother." Reading that passage I immediately thought of McCullough and how that institution—so redolent of bygone, honorable notions such as duty, obligation, and gentlemanly conduct—in a sense played the same formative role in my life as Lincoln's stepmother. My parents and McCullough together made me what I am today.

* * * *

I like to think that each of our minds contains a vault full of precious films of remembrance that we periodically extract and watch in the darkened theater of our memory. We are almost always the lead actor, director, and cinematographer for these films of recollection. And these films, no matter how imperfectly accurate and self-fashioned they may be, should be treasured, for they signify and validate our too-ephemeral lives.

One of my favorite memory films takes place during my first year at McCullough, during a third-grade class. Imagine a film shot in wistful black and white, evoking a Truffaut-like sweetness and empathy. It shows me sitting at my desk toward the back of the room, adjacent to a window that looks out over a faded, grassy courtyard. I am looking down while I do some schoolwork. I look up and then out the window, and I see something that I've only ever seen in the movies or on television: snow falling—big fluffy flakes of American snow.

Next thing I know, the teacher, Mrs. Kingman, is standing beside me. She looks down at me and, following my visual path, realizes what has so mesmerized me.

"Have you ever seen snow before, F.P.?"

"No, ma'am," I answer.

"Would you like to go out and see it?"

"Yes, ma'am!"

So she takes me by the hand, and as she leads me out of the classroom she asks the rest of the class to follow along. Without pausing to don our coats, a short caterpillar-like line of us winds down the hallway and out the door into the courtyard. Mrs. Kingman leads me to the center of the courtyard as the snow begins to fall harder. My classmates, in their striped pants and black-tie cadet uniforms, silently form a circle around me. I stand with my arms stretched straight out and my palms upturned, a little Cuban supplicant. I lean back slightly, crane my head way back, and open my mouth wide, shutting my eyes. The large, soft, wet snowflakes caress and tickle my palms and face. Flakes fall into my mouth and every once in a while I swallow. The cold snow tastes like a fresh new world, like the future, and I hear my classmates giggling and boyishly embracing my happiness.

Death of an Oriole

Well, bless my Natty Boh, Hon,
Don't you know, our uncaged Gracie done came
    home again,
Even though that North Carolina doctor advised
    her not to;
To my way of thinking, Hon, it was a crazy-odd
    trip for someone our age;
And her son, Earl, you know the lawyer one with
    the stuck-up Roland Park wife,
Called and described what transpired with our
    cherished free-bird friend.

She'd been staying down in Chesapeake Beach for
    going on two weeks, and there
She'd gone to remembrance-crowded places that
    made her smile through tears;
She'd smelled the kindly, brackish bay smells that
    she adored so dearly;
She'd tasted the sand-scented Proustian flavors
    that sated her famished memory;
And, Hon, she'd heard the secret seagulled sounds
    that set her soul to dancing.

But yet, Hon, she said she felt the pressing of a
    reproachful permanence

That did not seek or require her personal presence
    or sanction;

And don't you know, Hon, just when sweet-tem-
    pered, mother Maryland

Seemed to want to embrace prodigal Gracie in her
    absolving arms, our friend,

In her own damaged way, got all flustered somethin'
    awful and flew away.

The Gravel Incident

Our home in Cuba contained a looped gravel driveway. The roadway on which our house fronted wasn't very heavily traveled, but there was the occasional car that drove by. Every once in a while when Jorge and I were very bored, with absolutely nothing fun to occupy us, we liked to stand at one of the driveway's loop ends, take handfuls of the small gravel pebbles, and throw them at passing cars. Keep in mind that I was maybe five years old and Jorge six, and, considering how much gravel we could hold in our little hands and how far children of our age could throw, it was rare that the gravel we lobbed ever reached our target. When it did the driver most likely didn't even notice. Until one day. On that day one or both of us hit the target, and the target came to a screeching halt. And Jorge and I hightailed it into the house.

We were hiding behind the living room sofa when someone rang the doorbell and simultaneously banged on the front door. It must have been a weekend day, because my mother was home, and it was she who answered the door. We knew my father was not home.

We heard the man shouting angrily about the damage done to his car by gravel thrown by two boys he'd seen running into this house and how someone would have to pay for it if they didn't want him to call the police, etc., etc. My mother succeeded in calming him down and assuring him that he would be paid for the damage to his car. After he left we crept out from behind the sofa. My mother gave us a look of resigned clemency and said, "You know I have to tell your father. When he gets home I want you both to go into Jorge's bedroom and stay there. I will handle your father."

My father was a kind and affectionate man who, without complaint, shouldered the role of family disciplinarian that marriage to my softer, more lenient mother had assigned to him. When he came home that afternoon we did as our mother had asked. After a few moments of relative quiet, the ruckus began. My father bellowed and raged. My mother pleaded and cried for mercy on our behalf. After a few minutes of frightening clamor, she must have run away from him because suddenly she was in the room with us slamming and locking the door shut.

By the time he reached the locked door my father's wrath had reached its climax; his roaring and pounding could probably be heard for blocks. My mother at first leaned her back against the door straining to keep him from breaking it down. Then she could bear it no longer; crying uncontrollably, she fell to her knees a few feet from the door, still pleading desperately for him to let us be. Jorge and I were cowering behind his bed.

That's when Jorge peeked over the bed and, during a gap in the horrible din, said to my mother, "Mamita, please, let him in."

She hesitated for a moment; the look on her face was one of terror mixed with a mother's sympathy and powerless capitulation to the inevitable. She stood up, opened the door, and stepped out of the way as my father burst into the room with his boundless Spaniard's fury, found Jorge and me, and took the belt to us.

Chapter 4

ONE OF THE THORNY IRONIES of my life is that I only really got to know my mother after leaving Cuba and during the distressing period when she was coping with her health problems and her difficulty with adapting to life in the United States. Not that we weren't close in Cuba—my mother was always a very loving parent. It's just that in Cuba she was a professional person with a demanding career as an attorney, which, of course, took up a lot of her time. Considering how much time we spent with our nannies, it is not surprising that Jorge and I were extremely devoted to them. As I am sure is often the case for children of professional couples, for a time we were probably more affectionate with our nannies than with our parents.

After arriving in this country and during the couple of years when my mother did not work, she was able to spend much more time with Jorge and me. I grew closer to my mother during that time. As I watched her suffer and struggle with her failing health and the alien environment, my love and respect for her grew immeasurably. Through my daily interaction with her I learned that a great deal of her suffering was caused by the mundane, day-to-day things.

I do not know very much about my mother's family and her upbringing. I know that they were wealthy, and like most affluent Cubans of that era they probably employed a full staff of maids and cooks. Consequently, my mother never had to learn how to cook or do household chores. She certainly never had to do such things during her married life in our family home in Cuba. I imagine that once in the United States it was very trying for her, especially considering her poor health, to have to clean, iron, and cook. And, bless her soul, she was such a terrible cook! I remember my poor mother crying many times over her burnt rice and how she would scrape out the very worst-burnt kernels for me because she knew I liked the charred taste. I watched her struggles every single day, and I know she felt powerless and inept. And that just made me love her even more.

*   *   *   *

When I was in fifth grade my mother's cancer returned. We were still living at the Reisterstown Road apartment over the grocery store. She had recently landed a job teaching at a very tough inner-city Baltimore school, and that only made things more difficult. I recall her tearfully describing to my father how her unruly students mercilessly harassed her and showed her no respect. She started suffering from migraine headaches that afflicted her almost daily. During this time I saw my father's softer side through his constant attempts to comfort her and his unguarded displays of profound affection and devotion. He appeared so undaunted and solid but somehow so defenseless.

My mother's stays at Johns Hopkins University Hospital became more frequent and lengthier. When she came home from one particularly long stay at the hospital she looked so very frail and defeated. Her loving but labored smiles at Jorge and me tried to warn us of her imminent departure. She now had to remain in bed.

Since we could not afford a visiting nurse and my father could not absent himself from his teaching duties, Jorge and I took care of her on schooldays. We took turns missing school. I do not remember how long that went on. Days? Weeks? I do not remember. Maybe I have blocked it out. It was very difficult. She was suffering so much. I heard her moans and cries of pain. I helped her with her bedpan, removed it, and emptied it. I helped her wash herself. I saw her heartbreakingly bare and scarlet-scarred chest. She was always hot and sweaty. And for some unfathomable reason the doctor had ordered that her intake of water be very limited. I had to hear my mother pleading for water, and I had to deny her. It was very difficult. I was ten years old. I was never the same again. Nothing could really hurt me after that. Not for a long time, anyway.

La Vida No Es Sueño

Whoever said "La vida es sueño" must have
been an utter fool; or did I simply misunderstand
     him?
Life is not a dream at all; it is a stark Hobbesian
     reality,
but longer, interspersed with infrequent, fleeting
moments of luminous joy, like a fireworks show
you fondly but barely remember.

The child who lost his mother to cancer was not
     dreaming;
The woman, raped and defiled, was not dreaming;
Your daughter's smiles on Christmas Day morn
     were real.
The man wrongly imprisoned was not dreaming;
The mother of the terminally ill son was not
     dreaming;
Your wedding day, a blissful future beckoning, was
     real.

Life is not a dream or illusion at all; it is concrete-
     hard,
corporeal, callous, and gleefully cruel, like a child
who tears the wings off a fly for amusement.
But life can be as gentle as your mom's kiss on your
     feverish forehead,

and as glorious as your grandchild's first birthday
    party.

Welcome and savor the joys; be grateful for the
    visits of grace.

The Traveling Show

In the summer of 1963, the summer following our first year in Baltimore, my family took a road trip back to Miami. I imagine that the main reason for our going to Miami that summer was for my parents to visit with the Cuban friends they had left behind. However, I have a theory that, for my father, the trip's primary objective extended well beyond simply visiting old friends. I believe that for the Monarch in Exile, that irrepressible and incorrigible self-promoter, it was nothing less than (drum roll, please): THE ROMERO FAMILY'S TRAVELING SHOW OF SUCCESS IN AMERICA. And I have a photograph to validate my theory.

It is a color photograph taken while we were visiting Miami. It shows the four of us standing next to the passenger's side of a pristinely white 1962 Ford Thunderbird. Jorge and I are in the center, flanked by our parents; my mother is next to me, and my father stands by Jorge.

Exhibit number one of my theory's proof is the car. My father was always an avid car enthusiast, and one of the first things he did when he began teaching at McCullough was to buy the T-Bird, which at that time was a highly desirable luxury car. How he afforded that car I will never know. But there it is in the photograph in all of its Turtle-Waxed glory, shining like a chariot of success.

Exhibit number two is what we are wearing in the photograph. Please keep in mind that this trip took place in either June or July, and Miami can, of course, be swelteringly hot and humid during those months. I will begin with my mother. She is wearing a flower-printed dress that is just a tad too tight, nylon stockings, and high-heeled shoes. It is obvious that her hair's been recently permed and colored at a beauty parlor, as she was not normally so blond. She's dressed as if she is going to dine at some swanky restaurant, but she looks hot and wilted and is squinting in the sun's glare.

Jorge and I are wearing full-dress gray McCullough military uniforms, including the dress jackets, visored caps, and spit-shined shoes. Looking at the photo more closely I note that we both have good conduct and honor roll bars pinned to our jackets. To add to the pathetic absurdity of our appearance in that oppressive Florida heat, we are both standing stiffly at attention and saluting at the camera. We look like embarrassed tin soldiers.

My father, Señor Duende himself, is dressed like a seasoned Madrid dandy decked out to do some sporting on the town. He is wearing one of his natty Savile Row knock-off pinstriped suits, his cuff-linked shirt sleeves peeking out proudly from his jacket sleeves, and black-and-white wing-tip shoes. His black hair is Brylcreemed back, and you can practically smell the heady scent of his English Leather cologne. His stance is urbanely casual, with his left arm jauntily draped over Jorge's shoulder and his right hand in his pants pocket. His commanding gaze radiates machismo and cocky amor propio. The photo doesn't lie: My father is el hombre—el hombre who has succeeded in America.

Exhibit number three is our itinerary for the several days we stayed in Miami, and you'll have to trust my memory on this one. We must have visited at least twenty homes during our short Miami "vacation." I imagine that a slightly different version of the photo described above was probably taken at each one of our visits. During each visit Jorge and I, in our splendid military regalia, would march (yes, literally) into someone's living room to deliver the same coached statements to our parents' rapt friends about how much we loved McCullough Academy, how delicious the food was in the school's cafeteria, how our classmates' families were so wealthy, and how much we loved the marching and drilling. And, of course, I had to relate the story of experiencing my very first snowfall surrounded by my third-grade classmates. Without a doubt that was the Romero Family Traveling Show's triumphant highpoint of each visit. My parents' friends would clap with unrestrained Cuban gusto, exclaiming how that was the most adorably precious story they had ever heard. And each time at the end of my story I would glance over at Jorge, who always looked as if he was about to throw up.

Chapter 5

I AM HOLDING ONE OF my most precious possessions, a sympathy card given to me during Mr. Mitchell's math class by my fifth-grade classmates at McCullough shortly after my mother passed away. The card is full of scrawled signatures from classmates that I will never forget. Many of them were the same boys who two years earlier had helped me to celebrate my first experience with American snow. They also gave me a baseball glove, which I used throughout my Little League, Camp Bennet, Pony League, and high school baseball-playing days. I don't know what ever happened to the glove, but I still have my treasured card.

* * * *

I learned of my mother's death the day after it occurred. It was late afternoon, and Jorge and I were playing baseball with some friends on the field behind Lewis Building. A fellow student called out to Jorge and me that our father wanted to see us at the Clarks' house. Dr. Clark, who taught French, was my father's closest friend at McCullough, and he and his wife were always very kind to us. During my mother's most recent hospital stay they had invited us over for dinner several times. I will never forget the uniquely cozy and hospitable smell inside their campus cottage: a sweet fusion of Dr. Clark's pipe tobacco blended with cinnamon and baked apples. It was the soothing scent of sanctuary.

Mrs. Clark was waiting for us at the front door and led us into their living room. I saw my father sitting in a high-backed chair with two dining chairs placed in front of him. I thought it very strange that he was wearing dark glasses. He asked that we sit before him. He took off the dark glasses, and I saw he was weeping. In a trembling voice he could barely manage he said just above a whisper, "Mi hijitos, tu mamita se murió ayer. Ahora está con Dios." (My little sons, your mother died yesterday. Now she is with God.) And he broke down sobbing. Not knowing what to do, Jorge and I took turns hugging him. Then Mrs. Clark gently steered us toward the front door, saying, "Boys, your strong father will be fine; just give him some time. Please come back and have dinner with us in an hour or so."

Jorge and I walked out and made our way across campus, back to the baseball field behind Lewis Building. I was sort of numb, so I failed to realize that the shell-hard armor for which I had been fitted during my mother's illness and that I still wear to this day, even though it is much dented, was finally placed on me at that very moment. Jorge and I returned to our baseball game without having spoken a single word to each other.

* * * *

I will never forget that night, lying awake in bed at the McCullough apartment, wanting so badly to cry over my mother's death. But I could not do so. I tried and I tried. I even tried thinking about various sad things that would maybe generate the tears—as if anything could be sadder than a boy losing his precious mother. But I could not cry. And I did not cry. I did not cry when I saw her in the open casket and kissed her cold forehead. And I did not cry at her funeral. And I did not cry when she wasn't there for my birthdays or Christmases or baseball games or graduation or to sweetly kiss my daughter as she used to kiss me. And so to this day I have never cried over my beloved mother's death.

* * * *

As always, for Jorge and me things got back to normal fairly quickly. We were always busy with school and sports, and I was greatly enjoying living on campus and exploring McCullough's seemingly boundless fields and woods, lost within myself for hours at a time.

My father wore the dark glasses for several months, and I know he suffered much, longing for his wife and the mother of his children. I can only imagine what that stalwart yet imperceptibly vulnerable man must have felt at that time, having lost everything in Cuba and then his wife also, knowing he had to raise two boys by himself. Every single time that I require strength in my own less-troubled life, I think about my father and silently thank him for the lessons he quietly bestowed upon Jorge and me, showing us how to endure without complaint or bemoaning one's destiny.

The Monarch in Exile was as strong as a Galician ox, and there were many considerate people at McCullough, folks like the kindhearted Clarks and many others, who helped him recover from his grief little by little. And not surprisingly, there were several single ladies at McCullough—I especially remember one of the school nurses—who were very zealous in their thoughtfulness toward my father and in their well-intentioned but futile efforts to be motherly to Jorge and me.

* * * *

During the writing of this book and especially for this penultimate chapter on McCullough, I have contemplated deeply on my life during that period to try to discover within my sometimes uncooperative memory any noteworthy experiences or episodes that would shed some light on my personal trajectory and its significance. Of course, I have thought of many things of which I'd like to tell, but one very distinct memory appears to have bested the others in getting my attention. I believe my attention was compelled toward that memory because it recognized it as a portent of what was to follow in my life. It is a memory of something that happened in early winter of 1965, eight months or so following the death of my mother. I was in sixth grade.

It was during the athletics period at the end of the school day. I should point out that at McCullough it was not unusual for students from different grades to be on the same field playing a game of football, soccer, or baseball. I should also note that it was obligatory for all McCullough teachers to participate as coaches, referees, or monitors during the daily athletics period. My sports-phobic father absolutely loathed this part of his job, especially during the colder months.

On this particular day we were playing soccer. I remember seeing the Monarch in Exile looking rather woeful as he stood on the sidelines. Most likely he was shivering since he was walking in place to stay warm, clapping, and rubbing his gloved hands together, the hood of his sweatshirt tied so tightly you could barely see the grimace of discomfort on his face.

I wasn't cold at all, as I had been sprinting back and forth from one end of the field to the other. I remember having the ball passed to me; as I proceeded down the field with it, someone shoved me violently from behind, making me crash headfirst into the cold hard ground. Enraged by the assault, I jumped up immediately and easily identified the culprit since he was spitefully grinning at me. He was an eighth grader and much bigger than me. He raced down the field after the ball, not realizing that I was furiously chasing him. As he stopped to try to steal the ball from someone I leaped on his back and wrapped my arms tightly around his neck. He lost his balance, and we fell together. As we lay on our sides I loosened my left arm and grabbed for his throat with that hand. Having achieved a good grip on his throat I squeezed and squeezed until several teachers, including my father, managed to pull me off of him. Having been yanked back up on my feet, I glared down at him still on the ground and saw that he was crying. I laughed at him as loudly as I could.

The Soirée
(Hats off to Charlie D. and Bobby Z.)

The Future, arriving like a blissful imbecile,
Graciously greets the approaching Past,
Who can't remember one damn thing;
Despair, delightfully dandified this evening,
Waltzes madly with a teary-eyed Joy,
Who woefully wears her widow's weeds.

And I, defiant, sing out to all the gathered guests:
"I don't know, but you know I will;
No, I don't know, but you know I will;
Yes, I don't know, but you know I will."
And within this edifice, decaying and disjointed,
No one bothers to sing along.

Reason, genuflecting, weakly whispers mea culpas,
While being spoon-fed by a failing Faith,
Whose ashen hair is clearly thinning;
And over in a corner, Evil, so innocuous and so cute,
Flirts with the disingenuous Good,
Who's oh so vile and dressed to kill.

And I, defiant, sing out to all the gathered guests:
"I don't know, but you know I will;
No, I don't know, but you know I will;
Yes, I don't know, but you know I will."
And outside in the distant early dawn
Someone begins to sing along.

The Hognose Epiphany

The sketch I hold in my hands, drawn forty-odd years ago, is of a speckled snake, half coiled and half erect, rearing its head, with its menacing cobra-like hood spread wide, its forked tongue frozen mid-lick. I remember the actual snake's histrionic hissing, which startled me at first, until I recognized it was a hognose by its goofy upturned snout and its pitiful pretense.

It was during final-exam week at McCullough that I encountered the snake. One day during a break between tests I strolled across the now-dormant playing fields as nesting killdeer needlessly performed their doleful broken-wing dances for me. I strode past Doc Sullivan's duck pond and into the woods I loved and understood so well.

The path on which I tread was soggy and tadpole-puddled from the heavy spring rains. A Baltimore oriole flew back and forth across the path as if someone were playing catch with an orange. The Maryland woods were a May-scented, green-tinged, and irresistibly alluring distraction for an eleven-year-old who lived to

stalk and capture snakes, mudpuppies, butter-
flies, and moths.

When the hognose and I first spied each
other it lay in the middle of the path, but not
for long, as it tried to make its grand escape
stage left. But before I could pounce, it turned
and spread its hood, hissing as in a Kipling
story; but, like a mongoose, I knew my prey
and its tricks well. So I took a few steps toward
it. Appearing embarrassed, the snake collapsed
and seemed to be dying, snuffed out by nothing
evident.

The thespian snake, now enacting its
tragic death scene, rolled over on its back, its
tongue protruding. The dramatic little char-
latan just lay there! Knowing its sham, I hid
behind a nearby tree, occasionally peeking out
at the supine trickster. Obviously thinking that
the stage curtain had fallen and the play ended,
the snake rolled back over, and without taking
a bow, slithered into the thick brush.

I recall doing a quickstep back to class,
late—demerit-laden late—and with my spit-
shined shoes splattered with mud, but with my
spirit quite pure. I reflected on my father, the
Monarch in Exile, who had taught me so many
lessons, one of which was that the best way
to keep life from ever becoming too frightening or daunting is to prepare for it well—as I
had prepared well for the comically theatrical
hognose.

Chapter 6

My last two years at McCullough were very happy. I felt very much at home living on campus, and my life was safely structured while also filled with freedom. I spent as much time embracing the wide-roaming solitude allowed me as I did reveling in the dorm-room camaraderie of my many boarder friends. It was an incomparable time during which I learned one of the most important lessons of my life: to love and savor the simple, modest pleasures that make life so grand and that have brought me such immeasurable joy—books, music, friends, baseball, and a well-tempered enjoyment of one's own company.

Jorge and I were thriving at McCullough as we were very well-rounded individuals, and at McCullough achieving a salubrious balance between good citizenship, intellectual pursuits, and sports was heralded as the ultimate ambition of every cadet. In our last year at McCullough, Jorge was promoted to the prestigious military rank of captain and I to the less exalted but respectable rank of platoon sergeant. Both of us were doing well with our schoolwork, consistently scoring A's and B's in most of our classes. And both of us were earning reputations as the school's prospective athletes of the future: Jorge as a quarterback in football and shortstop in baseball and me as a baseball pitcher.

* * * *

During these years I developed a close friendship with a classmate named Rusty Vanderpool, who came to McCullough when we were both sixth graders. Rusty was a boarding student from Reading, Pennsylvania. I had never met anyone with the splendid zest for life that Rusty exhibited, and as I have always been passionate about anything close to my heart—to the occasional annoyance of others—it wasn't surprising that we soon connected over a shared enthusiasm: music.

Since I'd watched the Beatles on *The Ed Sullivan Show* in 1964, rock and roll music had become an integral and indispensable part of my life, as it still is. I developed an insatiable hunger for rock and roll and its older, less rebellious sister, soul music. Just about every penny of the weekly allowance provided to me by the Monarch in Exile went toward the purchase of records, both 45s and LPs. And since my family rarely left the McCullough campus, it was Rusty who bought the records for me during his weekend visits home to Reading.

During the period of 1965–1967 we spent countless hours in Rusty's dorm room listening to music on his compact record player. It was a splendid time for music; from the British Invasion to the Motown sound to the San Francisco music scene, we were obsessed with it all. And as will become more evident later in my story, my love of music and, in particular, playing music in a band, brought me much bliss, many unforgettable friends, and more than a few rousing adventures.

* * * *

One evening when Jorge and I returned to the apartment after spending a few hours practicing our baseball batting and pitching—using a regulation bat, tennis balls, and a chalked strike zone on a wall in the old McCullough gym—we saw Mr. Mitchell walking away from our apartment and my father at the door. We exchanged greetings with Mr. Mitchell as he left, and we went inside. The Monarch in Exile asked us to sit at our dining table, which was rarely used as such, since we ate most meals at the school cafeteria.

Before I continue, I'd like say a few words about Mr. Mitchell or, as we usually called him, Coach Mitchell. You may remember Coach Mitchell from earlier in this story as it was in his fifth-grade math class that my classmates presented me with a sympathy card and a baseball glove following the death of my mother. Coach Mitchell was both the varsity football and baseball coach at McCullough, and since his teams had brought the school much glory over the years with their winning ways, he was a revered and popular figure on campus.

The following is what my father related to us at the dinner table that evening. Coach Mitchell told him that he'd been following Jorge's and my progress in intramural sports over the last several years. He was also aware of our great success in the Pikesville Little League, where we led our team to the championship the previous year. (I still have the *Pikesville Gazette* article, "Romero Brothers Lead Cubs to Championship.")

Coach Mitchell had asked my father whether we would be interested in spending the upcoming summer at Camp Bennet, a boys' camp in New Hampshire that operated a football and baseball training program. Coach Mitchell and other Baltimore-area coaches annually selected several athletes from their respective schools to attend Camp Bennet during the summer months. And Coach Mitchell had selected us to represent McCullough that year.

We were absolutely thrilled and flattered by Coach Mitchell's proposal, especially considering how young we were. At that time, 1967, Jorge was fourteen and I was thirteen—years away from playing varsity sports. But my father soon deflated some of our excitement by informing us of one catch to Coach Mitchell's proposal, one major condition for our attending Camp Bennet. Since sending us to the camp was very expensive and we certainly could not afford it, Jorge and I would have to earn our camp fee by working as kitchen help at the camp's dining hall during the entire time we were there. And of course, the Monarch in Exile had agreed to Coach Mitchell's proposition.

And how did Jorge and I react to this decision? With our smiling-chameleon attitudes, of course; we never expressed one single word of dissent. It's not as if we hadn't worked before. The previous summer we had worked at the school's horse stables, mucking stalls to earn horseback-riding time. And that same summer we had worked for a full week at the Maryland State Fair in Timonium, strolling throughout the fair hawking schedule catalogs for about ten hours a day.

* * * *

We rode with Coach Mitchell and his wife during the day-long drive to Camp Bennet, which was located just outside of the town of Wolfeboro, New Hampshire. One recollection of that trip is hearing "See You in September" by The Happenings on the car radio quite a few times. Funny how things like that can stay embedded in your mind.

Camp Bennet, which no longer exists, consisted of several hundred acres of thickly pined New Hampshire woods, sports fields, and beach on the vast Lake Winnipesaukee. Boys were assigned to the half-dozen cabins according to which team they belonged: blues or grays. The largest building at the camp was the dining hall, which of course we would get to know well. I will not spend a lot of time describing the day-to-day camp life and activities, which were typical of a summer camp, because Jorge and I, along with other camp working staff (except counselors) did not get very involved with the campers' daily activities.

One could say that Jorge and I found ourselves in what today is referred to as a win-win situation—that is, if you have a glass-half-full disposition like we did. As long as we satisfactorily performed our jobs in the dining hall, we could enjoy any of the camp activities in which we wished to participate, time permitting. However, we were not obligated to adhere to the campers' rigorous activity schedule, lived mostly unsupervised in a separate cabin that housed only working staff, and had the freedom to do as we pleased as long as we did our jobs and participated in the formal sports training camps, which, of course, we loved to do.

Our dining hall duties required that every day we assist at all meals with the food preparation as well as set the tables, serve the campers and counselors, clear the tables, and wash all pots, pans, and dishes. (All hail Hobart, the mighty conveyor dishwashing machine!) We usually worked for two to three hours each meal, for a total of eight or so hours per day. The work was demanding and exhausting since at every meal we raced from one task to the next, making sure the campers and camp staff were kept happily fed and the two cooks—our bosses—were satisfied with our work efforts.

Clearly, between working and the daily sports practices Jorge and I were kept crazy busy. Oh, the boundless energy and resilience of youth! And I always made time to explore the endless woods, hunting for types of snakes not found in Maryland and spending time on the lake swimming or canoeing. It was a glorious summer of exploring life outside the comfortable confines of McCullough, and I felt a little guilty at not missing the Monarch in Exile very much.

Maricela

My father was very kind, generous, and paternal to my cousin Maricela during the almost two years (1965–1967) she stayed with us at our McCullough dorm-building apartment. He had invited Maricela to stay with us while she completed her college education at Towson State College. She had been living in Miami with her parents, my Tía Lucita, my mother's older sister, and my Tío Pepe. My father paid for her flight to Baltimore, her school tuition, and all of her expenses while she lived with us. During her time with us she had her own bedroom, while my father, Jorge, and I shared the other bedroom, with me once again sleeping on a foldout cot. Maricela brought a woman's soothing touch, voice, and warmth to our dismally masculine abode.

I know that by the time she left us my father had grown to feel deeply betrayed and disappointed by Maricela for reasons that were willfully his own. However, I believe that much of his heartache and anguish may have resulted simply from the fact that the Monarch in Exile, despite all of his hard-earned worldly wisdom, had absolutely no clue as to what he was getting himself into when he invited that beautiful, lively girl to live with us.

Maricela was a twenty-year-old, dark-haired, black-eyed beauty, whose unambiguous allure was both intimidating and welcoming, the latter especially so when she gave you one of her playfully tender smiles. She was a happily Americanized Habanera, sugarcane sweet but Gringo-independent. It seemed that her Cuban aristocratic dignity often lost its ongoing struggle with her girlish impetuosity. In most ways she was still a coltish teenager; she mooned over Sam Cooke and the Righteous Brothers, couldn't bear to miss her weekly *Shindig!* or *American Bandstand* television shows, and, with her impressive physique insolently stuffed into pink pedal-pushers and a front-knotted blouse, she would watusi or boogaloo for what seemed like hours to the blaring top-forty radio hits on Baltimore's WCAO. Eventually she would feign utter exhaustion and dramatically collapse on the sofa like a telenovela version of Elizabeth Taylor, all the while giggling like a schoolgirl.

While Jorge and I, for both familial and other perfectly natural but less proper reasons, were thrilled to have Maricela living with us, I don't think it took the Monarch in Exile long to begin questioning the wisdom of his generous invitation. The gushy love notes and other passion-filled missives to Maricela that were soon being slipped under our apartment's door on a regular basis—that were often intercepted by my father—were the first hint of trouble. But these letters of desperate adoration from lonely, love-starved cadets, no matter how worrisome and annoying for my father, were trivial in comparison to the campus scandal caused by her alleged affair with a McCullough teacher.

His name was as apropos as it was alliterative: Fabrizio Favoritti. He taught Italian and Latin to McCullough juniors and seniors. If Maricela was a budding Elizabeth Taylor, he could have passed for a Marcello Mastroianni stand-in, dashingly handsome, emanating an old-world elegance. The fact that he drove a cherry-red Alfa Romeo, wore dapper Continental attire, and spoke with a thick, lusty accent only added to his undisputable appeal. It was bruited about campus that Fabrizio, who I imagine was in his mid to late thirties at the time, had been involved in dalliances with several of McCullough's lady teachers.

As an occasional confidante to Maricela, I learned that her infatuation with Fabrizio was immediate and intense, swiftly becoming a merciless master over her conscience and judgment. She was an inexperienced and ardently romantic Cuban girl encountering the first grand passion of her life. On the other hand, the Monarch in Exile believed that

Maricela was still the dutiful, chaste Catholic-
school lass he had watched grow up in Cuba.
And being somewhat of a stranger to empathy,
he was blindly unaware of the supremacy that
such a young girl's heart holds over her will
to behave virtuously or, at the very least, dis-
creetly.

In describing Maricela's involvement
with Fabrizio, I used the words "alleged
affair," as I have no definitive knowledge of
what occurred between them. Of course I
heard the rumors that my classmates excit-
edly but uneasily repeated to me, not knowing
whether they were irritating me or nourish-
ing my own adolescent prurience. I heard the
stories about how Maricela and Fabrizio had
been discovered embracing passionately inside
the Alfa Romeo at various secluded locations
throughout the campus. I also heard about the
time they were spotted hand-in-hand entering
a Reisterstown Road bar, even though it was
illegal for Maricela to do so at her age. And I
recall the weekend that Maricela purportedly
spent at the home of a college friend. When
she returned to the apartment on Sunday
evening my father instantly and forcibly pulled
her into her bedroom, and his shouting and her
wailing became so unbearably noisy that Jorge
and I escaped from the commotion to go shoot
baskets at the school gym.

I certainly never questioned Maricela

about the true extent of her relationship with Fabrizio and by the time I grew old enough to have the resolve to ask my father about the matter, I realized he did not wish to discuss Maricela at all, least of all with regard to her having embarrassed and angered him so greatly. For you see, the Monarch in Exile, even though he enjoyed presenting himself flamboyantly (within reason) and did not object to attaining a particular kind of self-serving notoriety, could never, ever countenance the black cat of scandal crossing his noble path. His dignity and integrity could not be challenged so publicly without grave consequences. And so his swift actions in loco parentis were unequivocal and tyrannical; he forbade Maricela from having any further contact whatsoever with Fabrizio and henceforth controlled her socializing with puritanical monitoring.

I believe that my father did exactly what he thought Maricela's parents would have wanted him to do and what was ultimately in her best interest. I do not think he was overly keen to assume Tío Pepe's and Tía Lucita's role as Maricela's parents. However, I think he justly deemed that Maricela's parents, who pointedly refused to learn to speak English or abandon their undying dream of returning to Cuba in the very near future, were having enough of a difficult time in Miami without having to suffer further apprehension due to their daughter's romantic shenanigans with a considerably older, reputed lothario. I do not think Tío Pepe or Tía Lucita ever found out about Fabrizio.

When the 1966–1967 school year began, Fabrizio Favoritti was no longer a member of the McCullough faculty as his contract had apparently not been renewed. Maricela continued living with us and graduated from Towson State in the spring of that year with a bachelor's degree in education. She never explicitly showed any rancor toward my father during her remaining time with us, but it was obvious that their relationship was irreparably damaged. Since her exuberance and joie de vivre were so innate, she remained outwardly unchanged and unfailingly cheerful during that last year with us. However, every so often late at night, when using the bathroom that separated our bedrooms, I could not help but hear Maricela's heartrending sobs.

Chapter 7

I HAVE ALWAYS HAD AN affinity for scoundrels, and Little Jack was the first scoundrel I ever met. Considering my naïveté at the time, I'm not quite sure I realized then that he was a scoundrel, but I certainly do now.

We had two cooks named Jack in Camp Bennet's kitchen. Consequently the older head cook was called Big Jack and the younger assistant cook was dubbed Little Jack.

I think I can describe Big Jack pretty accurately in six words: retired navy, tattoos, crew cut, and gruff. He treated the kitchen staff with drill-sergeant severity at work and cranky indifference outside of it, and I childishly hated him for a good part of the summer until he had a mishap with a meat slicer and lopped off half of his thumb. The way he handled the situation with such impressive sangfroid, calmly asking that one of us call for an ambulance while the blood ran down his thick arm, made me appreciate the fact that this was a man who I may not like but I should not hate. I made it a point to show him a lot more deference after that.

I never learned much about Little Jack's history prior to my working with him or why he ever became a cook at Camp Bennet. From what he related to me regarding all the different places he'd lived, I now assume he must have been a drifter type, a rolling stone. He must have been in his late twenties when I knew him. He was short and skinny but muscular, with longish, wavy dark hair and gray eyes that always squinted as if he had a headache or was thinking real hard about something. With the squint and his obviously once-broken nose, he wasn't exactly handsome, but I'd say he was attractive.

Little Jack was one of those guys other men are drawn to because of their convivial, ne'er-do-well charisma and whom certain women adore for whatever reasons such women adore roguish and clearly damaged guys. I know that he drove his motorcycle into Wolfeboro just about every night and invariably returned with tantalizing tales of escapades with his "dates," many of whom he said were married. I thought he was the coolest guy in the world.

I don't know why he befriended me that summer other than maybe he appreciated that somebody admired him as much as I so genuinely and shamelessly did. He would drive me on his motorcycle into Wolfeboro on dateless nights to catch a movie or visit the drugstore malt shop. And whether at the malt shop or at the cabin, we talked incessantly as I tried to mine his rover's wisdom. Little Jack provided my first cigarette (Winston) and my first drink of alcohol (Gilbey's gin), and he told me much about girls. And when my roommate, who was a jerk, started bitching to everyone about the snakes I kept in jars and boxes in my room, Little Jack, with just a trace of menace in his voice, persuaded him to keep his mouth shut.

Little Jack was also a music lover, and that Summer of Love was one of the greatest ever in the history of popular music. In his cabin room we cranked up the volume on Hendrix, the Doors, Jefferson Airplane, Janis Joplin, the Who, and many other greats who today, sad to say, are indiscriminately and collectively tossed into the cobwebbed category of Classic Rock. To this day, I can't help but think of Little Jack whenever I hear Procol Harum's "Whiter Shade of Pale," our favorite song of that summer.

And something that shocked me at the time, because I had not yet grasped the truth that most of us are walking contradictions, was how deeply well-read Little Jack was. As a cocky bookworm I assumed that I had read more books than a peripatetic rascal like Little Jack. But I soon learned how wrong that assumption was. I never saw Little Jack more content than when he sat on the edge of his cot and, looking all squinty-eyed and serious, discoursed like a tenured professor on his love of literature. This hipster autodidact spoke to me of Proust, Joyce, Faulkner, and other greats, but mostly he spoke of the Russian literature with which he was obsessed, and especially of the writer he called "The Master," Dostoyevsky.

Now, of course, Little Jack's erudition was well over my thirteen-year-old head, and when he loaned me his tattered copy of *Crime and Punishment*, I didn't read but half of it before I was thoroughly defeated by the peculiar Russian names and the unbearable weightiness of the whole thing. But Little Jack had planted a seed. Years later I took up Dostoyevsky on my own, and reading his works became one of the enduring pleasures of my life. And to think that I have a squinty-eyed, complicated scoundrel like Little Jack—whose last name I don't even remember—to thank for that amazing gift.

Sadly, Little Jack was fired from his job at Camp Bennet before the end of the season. The scuttlebutt had it that he'd been arrested following a bar fight in Wolfeboro. There were also murmurings that he'd stolen money from Big Jack. No one other than the high-level camp directors seemed to know the truth. Somehow I sensed that Big Jack also knew the truth and for several days I pleaded with him to tell me, but even when I went out of my way to tell him how greatly I fancied his personal pièce de résistance—creamed chipped beef on toast—he still wouldn't tell me.

Big Jack's reticence about Little Jack's hasty departure did not surprise me, but I was puzzled to find that he began to treat me more kindly, showing an apparent interest and concern about my daily non-work activities. His new, solicitous manner with me was openly protective. To my mind, he behaved as if he had detected something to which I must have been blind, something concerning Little Jack's growing influence on me, something for which Big Jack felt he needed to atone, as if he'd been remiss in his duty to safeguard my character. In hindsight I now believe I understand the reasons behind Big Jack's odd change toward me, and it makes me wonder whether that cagey, crotchety old cook hadn't himself orchestrated Little Jack's ouster from Eden.

* * * *

I am fast approaching the end of my Camp Bennet section and I realize I have yet to write about the most important reason Jorge and I were at the camp in the first place: sports. I will focus on baseball since the football training camp that Jorge attended was just that, a training camp, and did not include games or any type of competition. In the baseball camp we actually formed a team that played against other camps in the area. So, I'll stick with baseball.

Jorge and I were the youngest boys in the baseball camp. Most of the other boys were either juniors or seniors in high school. However, when after a few weeks of practice the starting lineup was announced, both Jorge and I were on it. It seems that Coach Mitchell, who was not the only coach, certainly had a lot of confidence in us. Since an older and more experienced boy was chosen to start at shortstop, Jorge was assigned the position of catcher so the team could still benefit from his fine batting skills and his rifle arm. Even though Jorge had never caught, being the great athlete that he was, it didn't take him long to become an outstanding catcher.

The coaches chose me and a senior from Tillman School (McCullough's greatest sports rival) as the team's pitchers. Of course, I was tremendously pleased with the situation, although I recall that I was somewhat intimidated by the thought of being so much younger than my teammates. What really made me happiest, however, was getting the opportunity to have Jorge as my catcher—a Romero brothers battery!

We had an excellent team and beat every camp team we played. Jorge led the team in just about every hitting statistic, and I won more games than the Tillman pitcher. And now I beg the reader to please indulge me and permit me to brag a little. C'mon, you were all kids once!

I recognize that most people know what pitching a no-hitter in baseball means. However, to make sure I've covered all my bases (pun intended) it is a game wherein a pitcher does not allow any hits by the opposing team during the entire game. I note, however, that one can pitch a no-hitter but still allow opposing team players to get on base via walks or defensive errors. A no-hitter is something every pitcher dreams of achieving. But, there is an even more acclaimed achievement for a pitcher: a *perfect game*—that is, a no-hitter in which no opposing player reaches base in any way!

So, please allow me to return to my vault of memory films and extract one of my very favorites. In that sweetly transitional summer, teeming with lessons of independence and bountiful bliss, during which I needed neither armor nor chameleon camouflage, during which the very highest peaks of my happiness were not shrouded by a single cloud and there were no threatening tomorrows, on an early August day, in the team's last game of the season, with Jorge as my catcher and our undefeated season on the line, I pitched a perfect game! I could have died a happy boy right then and there.

* * * *

Before I close this section there is one more highlight of that wonderful and treasured summer at Camp Bennet I'd like to recount. Every summer was brought to a traditional end at Camp Bennet with a dance in the dining hall attended by girls from a nearby camp.

At that time, the only girls I had ever spoken to were daughters of McCullough faculty, some of whom lived on campus and whom Jorge and I would run into at the horse stables or the campus swimming pool. I do not believe I ever said more than one or two sentences at a time to those girls. And I had certainly never danced with one of those mysterious, inaccessible creatures. At McCullough I was scared to death of girls.

Of course I knew about the upcoming dance, and, although I remember feeling somewhat nervous, I also remember feeling a confidence that could only have been born of my having emotionally survived my mother's illness and death just two short years back, working my first real job, getting to know Little Jack, throwing a perfect game, and living independently all summer with older boys and men. I don't think I was very scared of girls at that particular point in time.

I went to the dance, danced most of the evening with one particular girl to whom I took an immediate liking, chatted and laughed with her as if we were old acquaintances, walked out of the dining hall holding her hand, strolled down to the beach, and, standing on the pale-fired sand and listening to the pacifying sound of Lake Winnipesaukee's waves gently greeting the shore, I kissed a girl for the first time.

* * * *

On the ride back to Maryland with Coach Mitchell and his wife I felt a deep sadness at leaving Camp Bennet, which in a few short months had become a place of life-long importance and remembrance. I also felt the expectant joy of going home to McCullough.

When we arrived at McCullough and pulled into the parking lot for Kyle Building I saw my father standing next to his black Mustang. Jorge and I got our gear out of the Mitchells' car trunk, said thank you and goodbye to the Mitchells, walked over to our father, and by turn hugged and kissed him. As Jorge and I turned to head toward the building and our apartment, my father stopped us and asked that we get in the car. Once inside, from the backseat I asked, "Where are we going, Papi?" He replied, "Hijos, I am driving us to our new home. It is in Prince George's County and I think you will be very happy there."

To be fair to the Monarch in Exile, there had been some talk during the previous school year about us leaving McCullough. Both Jorge and I were aware of how very unhappy our father was at McCullough. We knew and accepted the fact that he deserved better. He wanted to teach at the college level, and we knew that he'd applied for a position at Prince George's Community College.

Having said that, we did not know that any decision had been made and in his letters to us at camp he never mentioned having made a decision. There would still have been several weeks left of summer after our return from camp and if a decision were to be made I guess we figured it would be made—with some input from us—during that time period. How very naïve we were.

As we drove through the campus for the last time I looked back from the backseat and silently said farewell to Kyle Building, Lewis Building, Allen Building, Talbert Chapel, John McCullough's statue, the horse stables, the playing fields, the wonder-filled woods, the sweet unity of my beloved stepmother McCullough, my childhood, and my silly, irretrievable innocence.

A Few Words about the Upcoming Chapters

NOW IT BECOMES MORE DIFFICULT.

Looking back over my life, I can clearly distinguish several very critical transitional periods. During these periods there always seems to occur an argument, a dialectical brawl of sorts, between the current phase of my life and the advancing new phase. Now, I don't want to be waxing overly philosophical, but it seems that the current phase represented the *thesis* of the dialectic, and the new phase always served as the *antithesis*. And I knew that somewhere along the line the two would inevitably reach a rapprochement and coalesce to become a *synthesis*, for better or worse. When exactly that occurred each time is beyond me.

At this point in the book, with McCullough Academy behind us, our thesis is at home sitting on the couch relaxing, unaware that out in front of the house our antithesis has just climbed out of a taxicab and, grim-faced as a deathbed visitor, is approaching the front door.

* * * *

I am a firm believer in and proponent of free will. Therefore, I'd like to make it crystal clear to the reader that my behavior and actions described during the forthcoming chapters are solely my own responsibility. Such behavior and actions were not caused by my subconscious anger with God for "taking away" my mother or pent-up rage at my father for taking me away from my "stepmother," McCullough, or anything to do with any inane psychobabble, no matter what shape or form. I did what I did because I *wanted* to; it really is that simple. And I note that due to constraints of time and the fact that I don't want to beat the proverbial dead horse, what is described in the following chapters accounts for only a minor percentage of the unsavory—and irregular—things that actually took place. So, for the actions that will be included, as well as those that won't, I sincerely apologize to those whom I may have intentionally or inadvertently hurt, offended, marred, scarred, scared, upset, trounced, humiliated, or damaged psychologically or emotionally in any way and, of course, to their families.

* * * *

At the risk of sounding maudlin and melodramatic, I feel that it is incumbent on me at this time to announce the death of the F.P. Romero of the McCullough years. Not his literal death, of course, but the fact that he will no longer exist in these pages as the nerdy, bookish, sports-crazy, gentlemanly cadet, as the potential future West Point or Naval Academy graduate or future herpetologist or lepidopterist or historian or the guileless, trusting, ever-sanguine child who swallowed American snowflakes and thereby thought he tasted a fresh new world and who was graced with his mother's sweet, harmless nature. No, F.P. Romero did not die, but in the fall of 1967 he simply willed himself to disappear … at least for a while.

part two

El Joven—Dionysus

The Catbird Seat
(With all due respect to Red Barber
and James Thurber)

And so it seems
That everyone is feeling very dead inside,
Except for you, my friend;
And everyone looks ruined and so wretched,
Except for you, my friend;
And everyone is way too quietly desperate,
Except for you, my friend;
And all are strolling toward the slaughterhouse,
Except of course,
For you, my friend.

And in the meantime,
You're allowed to frolic and cavort;
And in the meantime,
You get to lick the cookie batter off your mom's
        spoon;
And in the meantime,
All the lovely lassies love you madly;
And in the meantime,
You're scoring the winning goal;
And in the meantime,
You've won the lottery, again!

Oh, my fortunate and god-favored friend,
You've been granted your much-merited ovation;
And without feeling even a smidgen of survivor's
    guilt,
You once again find yourself atop the catbird seat.

And so it seems
That everyone is fast-dwindling and depleted,
Except for you, my friend;
And everyone is too tangled in their terror,
Except for you my friend;
And everyone is dueling with their demons,
Except for you, my friend;
And all are so damn deathly afraid of dying,
Except, of course,
For you, my friend.

And in the meantime,
You've been given the keys to the candy store;
And in the meantime,
You're on safari with celebrities;
And in the meantime,
You're a hero to your own valet;
And in the meantime,
You're gamboling with the geishas;
And in the meantime,
You're voted employee of the month, again!

Oh, my fortunate and god-favored friend,
You've been granted your much-merited ovation;
And without feeling even a smidgen of survivor's
    guilt,
You once again find yourself atop the catbird seat.

Vikings on Harleys

What baseball and football players were to most boys growing up in 1960s America, bikers were for Seabrook boys. Seabrook boys considered bikers as their supreme, god-like heroes: long-haired, bearded, tattooed, pierced Vikings on Harleys. If they had had bubble gum trading cards of bikers, Seabrook boys would have traded cards of notorious renegades such as Dusty Jenkins of the Pagans, Snake Weaver of the Devil's Disciples, Buddy Parnell of the Satanic Outlaws, Crunch Turley of the Grim Reapers, and many other hell-raising heroes. Bikers were our only idols, our ultimate role models. And that is despite the fact that some of the ones based in Seabrook kicked our asses on a fairly regular basis. Like Cherokee Hatmaker, who never did like me for some darn reason and who throttled my ass severely a couple of times, but I still loved the thought of him. And I'll never forget how some years later Cherokee picked me up hitchhiking on a rural Maryland road. As I got into the old pickup truck, I recognized him. While I waited for the inevitable blow he glanced at me and growled, "Jesus loves you, brother" and smiled at me with brotherly and peaceful goodwill.

Twice a year a bunch of us bikers-in-training greaser boys would make the five-mile trek up Annapolis Road to Capital Plaza for the carnival, to which biker gangs from throughout Maryland would ride like proud warriors in full regalia, thirsty for booze, babes, and battle like civilization-starved mountain men at a spring rendezvous in the Rockies. My buddies and I would wander around the carnival, stalking our own personal heroes, gazing in desperate adoration at them and their magnificent motorcycles, and tacitly pledging our boyish allegiance to every damned thing they stood for: unquestioning loyalty, unmitigated meanness, unwarranted violence, and true American freedom. No wonder Seabrook boys loved to fight and commit evil.

Chapter 8

THE MONARCH IN EXILE WAS not one to make mistakes, but I believe he inadvertently made a real serious blunder in moving us to Seabrook, Maryland, just before the start of the school year in 1967. There were other places closer to his new college job to which we could have moved but he decided on an apartment complex in Seabrook because it was within walking distance of Wernher von Braun Junior High, a school that my father thought would be every bit as exclusive as McCullough Academy.

In all fairness to him, I imagine that his perception of von Braun Junior High was based on an overly hopeful syllogism that went something like this:

> There is a major NASA facility in Greenbelt, just up the street from von Braun Junior High. NASA's egghead scientists have children that need to attend nearby schools. Therefore, von Braun Junior High will be full of neophyte

NASA eggheads, ensuring that it is a high-quality center of learning for my sons.

What the Monarch in Exile failed to detect was the demographic nature of the town of Seabrook. Seabrook was proud of its hardcore blue-collar reputation. During the time we lived there much of its population was working class, made up of auto mechanics, carpenters, plumbers, electricians, truck drivers, and so forth. I imagine that very few NASA scientists lived in Seabrook and that very few of von Braun's students were the children of NASA scientists. In fact, many of the students at von Braun were what were then called *greasers*, most of whom were not very academically inclined but were much disposed toward violence and other types of wrongdoing. It is to those students that I was strongly attracted and to whom I gravitated like an abandoned Rottweiler to a pack of wolves.

* * * *

Choice—for better or worse, it is what makes life worth living. Nothing sings as beautifully of freedom as our personal choices; they are the Bel Canto arias of our freedom.

In anticipation of what follows I respectfully seek the assistance of a short poem by Henrik Ibsen:

> *To live is to battle with trolls*
> *In the vaults of heart and brain.*

To write: that is to sit
In judgment over one's self.

And when you sit in judgment over yourself one of the most arduous challenges awaiting you is the search for the reasons behind your personal choices. Some are quite easy to find as they are floating on top of the water right next to you; all you have to do is lift them out of the water and toss them into the boat. Other reasons are not as explicit since they are lying at the bottom of the murky, danger-laden water. You can hardly make them out, let alone comprehend their meaning. And now you're confronted with another choice: will you choose to take the risk of diving into the opaque water, swimming deep into the fear of not knowing what you will find and bring up to the surface?

* * * *

It was during the first few days in eighth grade at von Braun Junior High that it struck me that I had landed on a very different planet from McCullough Academy. For this was a planet mostly inhabited by a colony of greasers. And please do not misunderstand me; I'm not talking about Fonzie or John Travolta in *Grease* here. To borrow what someone once said about Lord Byron, these people were "mad, bad, and dangerous to know." Very dangerous to know, indeed, and worse yet to cross.

For those of you who are unacquainted with this breed, this now mostly extinct subculture of angry young men and women, I will try to enlighten you on their appearance and behavior. I'll focus here on the males as they were the first with whom I made contact or, to put it more accurately, who first made contact with me.

Males of the Seabrook genus of greasers, also referred to as Blocks, conformed to a rigid dress code that did not look kindly on deviations. Greaser boys wore skinny blue jeans with the cuffs rolled up several inches or baggier work pants, typically blue or khaki. For shirts they had to choose between bowling shirts, silk shirts, or Banlon shirts, never ever tucked in. Fitted t-shirts or wife-beaters were permissible outside of school. The socks they wore were silk and striped, sometimes worn under pushed-down white or gray crew socks, especially when wearing the requisite black Converse Chuck Taylor All-Stars. The other de rigueur shoe was the black biker boot, or shit kicker, a fine accoutrement for stomping on weaker males. The hair, of course, had to be slicked straight back with pomade or shaped as a pompadour or duck's tail. During cold weather three-quarter-length black leather coats were obligatory.

The greaser's attitude had to be one of uncompromising, born-to-be-wild cockiness mixed with an apparently unquenchable desire to do violence and bodily harm. Some of them had valid reasons for being angry but most just wanted to be so. Most greaser boys I knew wanted to grow up to be bikers or mechanics or, with luck, both.

* * * *

On the fourth day of school while walking down the hallway between classes I was approached by three greaser boys. The apparent leader of the trio, a boy named Spike Mandrell, got up in my face and asked, "Hey jerk, are you Block or Collegiate?"

I should explain that Collegiates were the von Braun version of preppies or sports jocks—such as my brother, Jorge, would become—and a very different colony than the greasers. They wore what at the time were called "mod" clothes—paisley shirts, tight white or black pants, desert boots or Beatle boots, longish hair—and were considered the greasers' only rivals for power. Of course, nerds and geeks did not have a poodle in that fight.

Spike's question took me aback since at that time I knew absolutely nothing about Blocks or Collegiates. Looking back, I guess that on that particular day I was unknowingly dressed closer to Collegiate than Block. But before I could answer Spike's question, he challenged me to a fight that very afternoon after school at a location he referred to as the Log.

I recall that during the few seconds that Spike was in my face presenting me with his challenge, I registered his actions as if they were in slow motion and I observed several things. First was the fact that he was one ugly son of a gun, with his flat, heavily pimpled face and reddish Brillo-Pad hair. Second, he was looking up at me from several inches below. Third, altogether, neither he nor his minions appeared all that fearsome or tough. So, with a mixture of McCullough resolve, foolish Cuban machismo, and the hubris that often attaches itself to a shell-armored individual, I accepted Spike's challenge.

I made a choice that day. I did not have to accept the challenge. Many other boys, maybe less proud and more thoughtful, would have made a different choice and stoically accepted the consequences, aiming for near-term bad but long-term good. I made my choice.

To be fair to myself, however, I need to point out that I believe my choice was largely made due to the somewhat unrealistic mindset I had acquired after five years of living a cloistered life full of books and honorable notions at McCullough. In accepting Spike's challenge I imagined that the fight would be a gentlemanly, McCullough-like scrap, maybe not a bout strictly adhering to the Marquess of Queensberry rules of boxing, but at least a close approximation. I was certain that no matter who won, both Spike and I would walk away from the fight feeling a sense of noble fellowship, knowing that we each had fought hard but with gallant sportsmanship.

To learn about the Log's location I sought the only friend I had made at the time, Greg Steiner, who was the type of kid who is so anxious to befriend you when you're new in school and whose friendship you gladly accept but cruelly discard a few months later when you callously feel you deserve better. I asked Greg what and where the Log was. He explained that it was a fallen tree lying across a clearing a few hundred feet inside the woods on the other side of the faculty parking lot. The Log was where the greasers congregated before and after school or when skipping class. It could be reached by a clearly visible path into the woods.

He was right; it wasn't hard to find.

Editor's Note: At this point it appears that F.P. ended Chapter 8 and skipped ahead to Chapter 13, the final chapter of the book. This is not unusual with authors, and according to Kahmeh Romero, F.P. liked to jump back and forth in the sequence of his story when writing his narrative. The only other explanation for the missing chapters is that they were somehow lost or misplaced and not included in the binders given to me. However, Kahmeh is certain that such is not the case. Her take on the missing chapters is that F.P. was extremely uncomfortable writing these particular chapters due to what Kahmeh described in an e-mail as F.P.'s "unfortunately angry, malevolent, and reprehensible actions" that occurred during the time described in these chapters, including unjustified violence, cruelty (to both humans and animals), and numerous acts of a criminal nature. She believes that F.P. felt great shame over the deeds that would be described in these chapters and avoided writing them until the time came at which he absolutely had to in order to finish his book.

Based solely on the Lost and Found narratives that I was provided and that follow, the missing chapters would presumably have recounted his remaining time in Seabrook, Maryland, during eighth and ninth grade (see "Butch P." and "Cathy Nap"); his year living in the rural town of Upper Marlboro, Maryland, during tenth grade (see "Brown

Station Road"); his two years living in the more urbanized Largo, Maryland, during a very tense period of interracial conflict throughout his junior and senior years in high school (see "Native Sons" and "The End of Béisbol"); and what Kahmeh calls F.P.'s "hippie, music-playing, vagabond years" (see "Trying to Remember 1973"). The final chapter also recounts that last period.

F.P.'s postscript and very affecting letter to his father, "Querido Papi," which in my humble opinion is a remarkably genuine and revealing document, I have placed toward the very end of the book.

Butch P.

Butch Pulaski—we often called him Butch P. for short—lived in the same apartment complex in Seabrook as I did. He moved there a few months after we did. It was just him, his father, and their white German shepherd, Queenie, living in the apartment. His mother had run off somewhere a few years back and his older brother, Junior, Seabrook's most determined but apparently most inept car thief, was again serving time for grand larceny. His father, Mr. P. to Butch's friends, was an unpleasant, surly, fat man who drank too much and constantly railed against the unjust world that had snatched away his pawn shop business. At the time that I knew Butch, Mr. P. had a job driving a Lays Potato Chips delivery truck and he was always complaining about that too. He was a real jerk and I tried to avoid visiting Butch whenever I saw Mr. P.'s delivery truck parked outside their ground-floor apartment.

Butch was a born comedian and one of the most wickedly funny people I ever knew. He just always cracked me up. Even our eighth-grade teachers at von Braun Junior High would find themselves reluctantly smiling when, in the middle of one of their pedantic talks on some highfalutin subject, Butch would shout out from the back of the class, "You're a liar!" And I still crack up when I recall the time when we had a joint appointment with the pompous school psychologist and Butch pulled the chair out from under the psychologist as he was sitting down. Jesus, that guy could sure crack me up.

Butch even looked comical, with his disobedient, thin blond hair always lying across his forehead no matter how much gel he put in it and his close-set blue eyes always smiling as if mischief were forever brewing in his brain. He had a prominent, sharp, and slightly bent nose and his mouth was permanently set in what I think he imagined was a sexy Elvis sneer. I used to kid him that he looked like a young but goofy Polish version of Robert Mitchum.

One mistake I think I made with Butch was to tell him of my father's grandiose concept about the exclusiveness of von Braun Junior High and his expectation about the high number of NASA scientists' kids who would be attending the school. Once I told him that, almost every single day he would harass nerdy boys walking in the halls. Making sure that I was watching, he would run up to one of them, dramatically point his finger at the kid, and yell at me in an exaggerated redneck accent, "F.P.,

F.P., is this one of them there egghead NASA kids? Watta you think, F.P.? Is he? Is he?" and so forth. The startled and frightened kid would just start walking faster to get away from us, most likely praying to God that this time we would not lay hands on him.

Butch was one of my closest greaser buddies and undoubtedly my favorite bullying partner. We collaborated on a considerable amount of aberrant behavior and shared a penchant for pushing the envelope of violence, both adhering to a fundamental principle of Seabrook self-defense that it is better to be considered crazy than tough. It didn't take me long to learn that his comic nature notwithstanding, he could, on the rare but memorable occasions when someone dared to rile him, transform into a rage-ignited animal that would put a brutal hurting on whoever crossed him. On more than one occasion I witnessed Butch assault someone much older and bigger and leave them on the ground a bloody mess. In modern lingo, Butch had serious anger management issues, the source of which a clueless school psychologist would never discover—but I happened to one day.

On that day, we had decided to skip our last two classes and were lounging on the couch in Butch's apartment, getting high by sniffing Carbona rug cleaner out of sandwich bags, smoking cigarettes, and listening to raunchy

Redd Foxx records when through the sliding glass door we spotted his old man's truck pulling up. I should note that Mr. P. was the type of parent, not at all unusual in Seabrook, who did not give a fig if his fourteen-year-old son smoked cigarettes in the house and since the Carbona bottle and the baggies were quickly thrust into our pockets, it wasn't as if we were freaking out. Although I do remember I was pretty tripped out on the Carbona, a mighty potent hallucinogen.

From the moment he entered via the sliding glass door it was obvious that Mr. P. was drunk. He walked unsteadily and slurred a cursory hello as he headed into the kitchen. He retrieved a can of Budweiser from the refrigerator and, after guzzling some down, stood glaring at Butch and me. "What the fuck are you two doing here? It's way too fucking early for you to be home from school."

"Pop, there was a fire in the school's cafeteria kitchen at lunch and they let us go early."

"You really expect me to believe that horseshit, you lying piece of shit? You're gonna end up just like your fucking loser brother."

"But Pop, I'm telling you the truth, I swear."

As an unambiguous clue to his position regarding his son's veracity, Mr. P. hurled his beer can at Butch, just missing him but striking a framed photograph of Pope Paul VI that hung on the wall behind the couch, splintering the frame's glass. And unfortunately for Queenie, she chose that moment to go into the kitchen to greet her master. In an instant and for no discernible reason, Mr. P. let out a roar and grabbed Queenie's back fur with both hands, lifted her up over his head, and, after balancing that very large dog there for a couple of seconds just like the great wrestling champ, Bruno Sammartino, used to do to an opponent, I swear the man pirouetted a couple of times and slammed the poor dog hard onto the kitchen floor. Queenie howled, bounced up, and took off toward the back of the apartment.

Butch flew off the couch, rushed toward the kitchen, and screamed at Mr. P., "Goddamn it, Pop, why the hell did you do that?"

Surprisingly swift for such a big man, Mr. P. grabbed Butch by the throat and slammed the back of his head against the kitchen wall. Then he held Butch's head firmly against the wall and punched him right square in the face—in the nose to be exact. Still stupefied by the Carbona, I gaped at this nauseating scene and saw the blood start streaming from Butch's nose.

As if recovering his dimmed wits, Mr. P. then backed off and did the weirdest thing: he started crying and sobbing, just barely getting out, "I'm so sorry, Butchy; I'm so sorry. Please forgive me, Butchy. Please, Butchy boy, forgive me. Please?"

Butch, who was staunching the bleeding from his nose using the bottom portion of his t-shirt, strode toward the sliding glass door, opened it, and, signaling to me with his eyes to exit, yelled at his father, "Fuck you, you fat, sorry-ass son of a bitch! Go to fucking hell!" And with that, we were both outside.

We walked around the corner of the building and leaned back side by side against the brick façade, trying to recover our ability to reason. After a minute or so I turned to Butch and asked him if he was going to be all right.

"Yeah, sure, why the fuck wouldn't I be?"

Following another minute or so, I turned to him again. "So what do you want to do now?"

Pulling his bloody t-shirt away from his nose he turned and looked at me with those smiling blue eyes that were almost covered with his disheveled hair and through that silly Elvis sneer of his drawled in his exaggerated redneck accent, "I reckon we can go find us one of them there brainy NASA kids and put a hurting on him real fucking bad. Are you with me, amigo?"

"I reckon so. But first, let's stop by my place and get you a clean shirt. After that we'll go to 7-Eleven and buy us a carton of eggs; that'll make it more entertaining."

"Fuck yeah."

Porfiry Petrovich Is in the House

So, what the hell are we supposed to do about the
damn guilt?
Should we try to confess it away via some grille-
profiled priest?
Or just ignore its incessant and brutal badgering?
Should we sweep it under the thick pile rug of
reason?
Sublimate it and fretfully await its inevitable con-
sequences?
Or should we become impervious to it like so many
Mansons manqué?

Really, just what the hell are we supposed to do
about the damn guilt?
They say the Jews invented it and creative Catho-
lics perfected it;
But I don't give much credence to that suspect,
priest-penned propaganda.
Did Socrates and Plato not feel guilt because they
knew nothing of Moses?
Or did they simply kill and bury the beast deep
within their academic cave?
And did the lean and hungry assassin know guilt
on that ideal March day?

So, what the hell are we supposed to do about the
damn guilt?

Of course, it's one thing when the source of the
guilt is suitably explicit;

But concealed by the ruckus of a cat-fight conscience, it's quite another matter.

And yes, I've read my Sophocles and St. Augustine
and, of course, Dr. Freud;

And I do concede that those thoughtful fellows had
some fairly valid insights.

But seriously, what the hell are we supposed to do
about the damn guilt?

Cathy Nap

Thank God or Dionysus or whoever for Cathy Napoli, aka Cathy Nap, who single-handedly and with the infinite chutzpah of the true Seabrook greaser girl, scaled the wall of my new-boy shyness, dropped down on the other side, and handed me the precious front-door key to the wonderful world of girls. And Cathy Nap could do this without worrying about what the other von Braun Junior High girls would say because she had dead serious greaser girl cred. With her teased up rat's nest of peroxide-blond hair, her Cabaret makeup, and her attitude of latent hostility, she could scrap and curse with the best of them, while, like most greaser girls I got to know, still maintaining an inner core of sweet, unapologetic femininity.

The world of Seabrook greaser girls was a treacherous territory one entered at one's own risk; if they personally didn't try to put a serious hurting on you, you can be certain their boyfriend or brother(s) would. Mess with them and those girls would have you running a virtual gauntlet of brothers and boyfriends that would sometimes seem interminable, with you always looking over your shoulder and running instantly whenever you heard a car brake hard.

Believe me, especially during my first year in Seabrook, before I fully earned my own street-combat cred, I did my fair share of tearing through backstreets and yards, fueled by sheer panic, and diving into any available hiding place, whether a trash dumpster, drainage pipe, an unlocked car, whatever. And I'll never forget the stomach-turning, cold-sweated primal dread that felt like a kick to the groin every time I was informed—usually by a smirking messenger—that some greaser girl's bad-ass boyfriend or brother was "looking for me." Those three chilling words would echo in my head, sometimes for weeks, like a hanging judge's sentence and I would drive myself crazy speculating on what the hell I had done to offend or annoy that particular girl. And I knew that sooner or later—at a party, or walking down the street, or entering a 7-Eleven, somewhere, sometime—I would be confronted with the vicious, beetle-browed barbarian of a boyfriend or brother that was "looking for me." (Mi amigo, la vida no es sueño; it is steel.)

Fortunately for me, Cathy Nap ranked high in the von Braun greaser girl hierarchy, and by bestowing upon me her stamp of approval, she accomplished the near-miraculous feat of making me, a goofy-looking, big-eared, bespectacled, awkward boy, appear more attractive as potential boyfriend material or as just a friend to other greaser girls.

It all started in eighth-grade geometry class, where she sat behind me, and within the first two weeks of school she was tickling the back of my neck with her pencil and passing me funny, flirty notes. To say the least, I was astounded by her forwardness. That's not what they taught us about girls at McCullough! And before long, I was invited to visit her parentless house after school.

Brown Station Road

He discarded the ridiculous nickname, the Tango Kid, given to him by his tough-guy greaser buddies, the very minute that high school became history. Later he looked back with bittersweet ambivalence on those years of shallowly buried anger, blindfolded searching, and unbridled recklessness.

While growing up in southern Maryland, home of tall tobacco, short-tempered machismo, and a million NASCAR dreams, he couldn't help but think of himself as a hapless anthropologist, dwelling with an indigenous people that he greatly loved, respected, and admired, but with whom he could never truly assimilate.

He recalls with mixed pride and regret, and the appropriate shame, the sustained backseat sieges he waged on dare-the-devil angels, more cunning and tactical than him, who eventually allowed the breaching of their stubborn walls, willing to lose the fleeting skirmishes but not the more protracted war of wills.

And he was quite perplexed as his repute grew with each so-called conquest, leading his pals to arrange for the laurel wreath and the triumphal procession, during which one of his chums sitting behind him in the muscle-car chariot whispered repeatedly in his ear, "You're no god, my friend; you're only human."

He remembers the midnight racing on Brown Station Road, the starting line near Fatback's shack, both gravel road shoulders packed with Schlitz-fueled future farmers of America and every Richard Petty wannabe in Upper Marlboro and beyond, flanked by their gaudy girls with their teased hair and danger-ous mouths.

He'll never forget one amazing night of racing, scared shitless as he rode shotgun with that crazy-ass ex-con Coleman Walker in his ominously rumbling Black Power Nova. Coleman blew the doors off the Lil' Woody GTO and his brother Jorge's fire-breathing Charger, even though he'd spotted each two car lengths.

He remembers the incessant, necessary fighting; the addictive adrenalin of striking blows of fury; and, maybe even better, the curi-ously aching allure of being struck, flirting with the pretty pain, and needing to explain away to his dubious father the ripe bruises and cuts, the bloodstained clothes in the laundry hamper.

Bloodstained clothes due to a hammer blow to his ear delivered at the Log or the beating he took from the Golden Gloves boxer or the brawl with the Bowie thugs on the frozen Miller Pond, ice-skate kicks stabbing his back as he pounded on some poor Hector's face, as if holding him personally guilty for his mother's death.

And he recalls how two lost years after high school, he finally faced reality and took a job as a county laborer, working with the Screw Crew, so-called since they got the nasty jobs. He worked with four roughhewn country black guys, who were damn tough on him at first, but who defended him later when it really counted.

And one transformative memory is branded on his mind of a particular day when the crew was picking up trash with pokers and plastic pails along the gravel shoulders of Brown Station Road. He recalls turning his head away whenever a car approached, praying to God that no old friend would recognize the Tango Kid.

Native Sons

It was the mouthy, freckled dude who stood in the hallway just outside the opened classroom door. Smiling, he glared death at me. I knew he was on our list, as I was on theirs, both of us probably pretty close to the top. They'd been trying to corner me for weeks, and there had been a few close calls.

I looked around the classroom. My classmates were either looking down or looking elsewhere, anywhere but at him. I was the only one looking at him. Mrs. Kershaw was oblivious to his presence as she was writing on the blackboard, something about the novel the class was reading; ironically, it was *Native Son.*

He was a big guy, muscular in a tight silk t-shirt. His Afro had a reddish tint which made the embedded blue pick stand out even more. I would later learn that his name was Nate Savoy, twenty years old, and not even a student at Thurgood Marshall High School. We made sure he got his; I remember we busted him up pretty good after the football game with Central.

I would not look away. He made the universal throat-cutting gesture and clearly mouthed, "You're a dead motherfucker." And he was gone.

It was 1970, eleventh grade for me. It was early in the school year, most likely October, and English was my last period of the day. I had no real friends in the class—none that would stand and fight beside me, anyway. I knew Freckles and his friends would be waiting for me when the bell rang, and I was dead meat.

Toward the end of the period I approached Mrs. Kershaw. I calmly explained my predicament while she looked at me as if I were trying to pull a fast one. I asked whether, seeing that we were on the first floor, I couldn't maybe open one of the back windows and slip out just before the bell. She smiled falsely at my request and said no.

I walked back to my desk and waited for the bell. Once it had rung, I followed my classmates out the door and into the hallway.

Imagine a cat surrounded and attacked by five or six large dogs. The cat will put up a hell of a fight, scratching and biting with unhinged fury, most likely drawing blood from some of its attackers. But eventually, the cat will be overpowered and mauled.

I was fully conscious of what was happening to me during the entirety of my mauling. As this wasn't the first time I'd been gang pummeled, I knew that after a certain number of strikes the face and body become fairly numb. So I don't remember feeling much pain while it happened. I do remember that while I was down, several of their girls took off their high-heeled shoes and struck me repeatedly on the face and the back of my head. I also remember that it took a month or so for all of the perfectly round purple bruises to fade.

El Fin de Béisbol

It is an article of faith with me that our worst mistakes, like ugly scars from knife wounds, even when concealed by our soul's self-made garments, stay with us forever. Their abiding presence is the price we pay for having invited them in the first place.

Not by happenstance, I believe, during one afternoon in late May of 1972 at a Thurgood Marshall High School baseball game, two of my most impactful mistakes manifested themselves in quite different ways. Early on in the game I became aware of the presence of one of the mistakes, and I'm fairly certain that that mistake was responsible, at least to some degree, for the later appearance of the other. And it's sadly comical to think about which of the two mistakes I've wasted more time dwelling on over the last forty-plus years.

"Romero, put your warm-up jacket on! Now!"

That was Coach Reilly, barking at me as usual about wearing my warm-up jacket in the dugout between innings pitched. As if after ten years of hurling a baseball thousands of times I didn't know how to take good care of my arm. Not the greatest coach ever, Reilly. I could never compare him with Coach Mitchell at McCullough, but he was a good man. He'd tutored me patiently for weeks so I could pass his Chemistry class the previous report period and thereby stay on the team. And he was incredibly tolerant of my prima donna antics as his ace pitcher: smoking cigarettes during practices, barely trotting when doing laps, absolutely refusing to ever slide into base, etc. I don't know how he put up with my crap.

After watching our second baseman, Greg Vitali, hit a single with no outs, I stepped out of the dugout and peered over its roof at the home-team grandstands behind it, hoping to see the Monarch in Exile finally in attendance at one of my games. There's always a first time, I thought. He wasn't there, and it hurt as this was the last home game of my senior year.

I looked up at Lauren and the little band of Budding Grove girls, who were laughing and carrying on in the top row. Watching Lauren laugh in such a carefree way I felt the vertigo of despair. My teenage heartache had recently been relentless and nearly incapacitating. We'd broken up a few months back over my serial cheating. In fact, I'd broken up with her, having grown tired of her annoying jealousy, her cloying, subservient ways, and her constant craving for my devotion. It took about a week before I'd awakened out of my narcissistic, macho dream world and recognized the magnitude of the mistake I'd made. How could I have been so stupid, so blind to what I had? On her part, as if it was the most natural thing in the world, she'd transformed overnight into a totally different, apparently more mature person, discarding me like some silly book she'd read and somewhat enjoyed, but certainly didn't wish to read again. Into the trash I went.

I'd been half insane ever since. Just about every night I'd been going out drinking and raising hell with my hoodlum buddies, most of them already out of school since they'd quit or been kicked out years ago. I'd even taken to stashing in my car bottles of Tango, a cheap faux-screwdriver drink I'd been imbibing for years. (Imagine a mix of lukewarm orange Kool Aid and crappy vodka.) I'd go out to the school parking lot throughout the day to take a few healthy swigs.

I stepped back into the dugout and resumed watching the game. Greg was still on first and there were now two outs. It was the bottom of the sixth in a regulation seven-inning game and we were ahead 2–1. An additional run would have meant some insurance padding as we went to the top of the seventh for our opponents' final at-bat. We and our opponents were tied for first place, so this game was of utmost importance. I was pitching a two-hitter and,

since I'd already beaten this team earlier in the
season, I wasn't all that worried.

There had been bad blood between our
teams for a while, for no ostensible reason
that I could remember. I recall that we didn't
like their coach because he was the only coach
in the division that wore an actual baseball
uniform, which we thought was phony as hell,
and because of the knack he seemed to have for
always attracting college and pro scouts to his
team's games. The scouts were there that day,
most likely to watch the other team's golden-
haired-boy star pitcher who was pitching that
day, and me. Over the season I'd had some
contact with several college scouts, mostly
casual conversations, nothing of any real significance, but never with scouts from the pro
teams.

As I watched, one of our better hitters,
Billy Bright, came up to the plate. Our opponent's pitcher soon had him at a count of no
balls and two strikes. As the next pitch was
delivered, Greg took off for second on a steal
attempt and Billy slammed a line-drive shot
that landed in the gap between the leftfielder
and centerfielder. As my teammates screamed
with wild joy at what was happening, I watched
as Greg began to round third base on his way
home and the other team's third baseman fla-
grantly stuck his foot out and tripped him. I
saw Greg fall headfirst onto the baseline dirt,

jump up almost instantly, and take down the third baseman with a running tackle. Simultaneously, a primal, irresistible rage like I'd never felt before, though I'd been murderously angry countless times before, engulfed my being like some satanic lord and I leaped out of the dugout and raced straight at the opposing pitcher, who had left the mound and was trotting toward Greg and the third baseman, who were wrestling on the ground. His back to me, the pitcher must have sensed my blitzkrieg assault coming since he was just beginning to turn his head toward me when I reached him. I locked my arms around his waist, lifted him as high as I could, and, with every ounce of brutish strength I could muster, I slammed him to the ground. I then stood over him and laughed loudly as he lay there crying out something about his arm.

And I'm sure it was just my imagination, but I thought I heard the two mistakes join in the laughter.

Trying to Remember 1973

The photo (who took it?) shows the three of us sitting on the edge of Sammy and Beth's waterbed, almost on the wooden frame. There's Lawrence, with his foot-high Afro, as always, with a guitar in his hands and James, looking like a hairy-chested Rapunzel, as always, with a bong in his hands and there's me, passing off as a goofier version of Frank Zappa, as always, with plenty of time on my hands. The air was hazy with weed smoke and most likely Jimi, Carlos, or Marley was blasting from the stereo. Between songs we could hear Sammy and Beth upstairs arguing loudly about how much longer we'd be staying with them in Denver.

Lawrence and I, like many of our friends, yearned for rock-and-roll stardom. So, we'd packed up our two-man band and hitchhiked from our ghetto apartment just outside of DC to Denver, the très hip city that summer of the ubiquitous "Rocky Mountain Way." A black hippie and me, looking like two freaks out of Zap Comix, thumbing rides across the United States—geez, we might as well have worn targets on our backs. We slept in farm fields and under bridges and barely survived on 7-Eleven food and fellow-freak kindness. Once in Denver, we played the bars nightly. On stage during the headlining bands' breaks, Lawrence's Strat wailed like Callas in Tosca and I beat on silly bongos.

Nothing much happened with our rock star dream, although I think I remember once meeting a really short Stephen Stills at one of the bars. There was some excitement brewing when we met Tennessee, the sociopathic biker who decided we'd become the Flyin' Wheels' house band *a la* Janice Joplin's gig with the Hell's Angels. Tennessee took a strange liking to me and gave me one of a pair of 14-carat gold earrings shaped like marijuana leaves, which I proudly wore for several years. He didn't get to wear his for long as he was imprisoned for clubbing to death a brother biker, thereby dashing our inane hopes of being the Wheels' house band.

And so we hitchhiked back to Maryland. Along the way I, like a fool, had rocks of Turkish hash taped under my belt, which (thank God) the Kansas cop who harassed us for hitchhiking didn't make me take off as he made us dump our duffel-bagged belongings onto the shoulder of I-70. Lawrence was greatly looking forward to seeing Jennie; me, I wasn't looking forward to anything at all as Michelle had moved out while we were gone.

Upon returning to our hell-hole apartment, with its broken windows and knob-less front door, I dove into a deep, ugly funk, in which I remained flailing until I was rescued by the unsinkable Holly.

The Departed Need Not Wave

Good-bye to all that, said a famous poet;
Good-bye to all that indeed.

Good-bye to the rushing life
That only brought slow results;
Good-bye to the ghetto language
That few could tolerate;
Good-bye to the catatonic silence
That only I could hear.

Good-bye to all that, said a famous poet;
Good-bye to all that indeed.

Good-bye to the futile violence
That was nothing but a drug;
Good-bye to the grandiose dreams
That veiled less worthy aims;
Good-bye to the self-formed ignorance
Of which only I had knowledge.

Good-bye to all that, said a famous poet;
Good-bye to all that indeed.

Chapter 13

THE CHRYSALIS BREAKS WITHOUT A sound and the very tip of a moistly crumpled wing, weakened by the effort but persevering, pokes out.

* * * *

My life as a "ghetto crow," as many of us mostly invisible denizens of Ellison Heights Apartments self-deprecatingly referred to ourselves, was coming to an end. It was November 1975, and I was moving out, making my escape.

My last act of churlish defiance against the apartment's landlord before my final departure from that wretched basement apartment, with its broken or missing windowpanes and the front door without a knob, was to stride into my bedroom, take a folding knife out of my pocket, and stab the bloated waterbed several times.

I lit up a joint as I watched the water spurt out. As I had already moved my conga drums and timbales to the new place, in the entryway I picked up the only other thing I was taking with me, a duffel bag full of my clothes, and walked out of the apartment.

* * * *

As I've alluded to in the two previous chapters*, during my three years at Ellison Heights, living in as many different apartments, and having to tolerate (and vice versa) more than a dozen crazily diverse roommates, I kept dancing gladly forward with the spinning, maddening contradictions: freedom and a craven fear of the future, hedonistic excess and (unwanted) Spartan deprivation, and recklessly immature behavior tempered by my new adult obligations. Now, it was time for the chameleon to once again generate newfangled colors and adapt to an unfamiliar environment. I knew it would be difficult and would not happen overnight.

On that day I wasn't particularly worried, but then again, I usually didn't worry much when I was stoned, which was most of the time. As I sat on the building's front stoop waiting for Holly to pick me up—I was again without a car and was hitchhiking to work and everywhere else except when Holly was available—I had some time to reflect.

I imagine that when a veteran theater actor retires, he most likely reminisces less about the stages on which he's performed than about the players with whom he's shared those stages. As I looked around me at Ellison Heights' cheerless, poorly tended tenement buildings, I realized that this place, with all of its great impact on my life, for good or bad, was merely a stage. What

---

*   *Editor's note: Two of the missing chapters.*

counted most were the other players, our not-always-happy band of bros, my fellow explorers of this new-found land teeming with personal choices.

I thought of the friends we'd lost over the last few years, those more foolish or less fortunate (or both) than the rest of us. Jimmy Albertine, the tough scrapper turned David Bowie glam queen—he kicked like a mule, all right—with his high-heeled shoes, midriff shirts, and sequined eyes, died *a la* Hendrix; he drowned in his own vomit one night after mixing too many Quaaludes with Jack Daniels. (I'd been luckier, as Holly may have saved my life one night when she was awakened by the sound of me vomiting in my sleep and kept me conscious long enough for me to recover from my Quaalude and Bacardi stupor.)

Flaco Alvarez, the loco-ass Nicaraguan, had been an extraordinarily gifted drummer whom I visited at his Ellison Heights apartment just days before he died. He had wanted to show off the new set of Ludwigs he'd bought with money his recently deceased uncle had left him; apparently, he'd copped some bad heroin with the same money.

And I thought of one of the most unique, impulsive, and frustrating friends I ever had, Johnny Buckmaster, our very own Falstaff, who made us roar with stoned laughter with his strutting Mick Jagger imitations. He once had the audacity to steal my television, which I sought to retrieve by breaking into his apartment. Instead of taking back my television, I lifted a pound of his weed, sold the weed in one-ounce bags over the next few days and used the money I'd made to buy Bob Marley concert tickets for everyone, including him. Johnny, crazy violent on the angel dust he'd been smoking, was shot to death by a DC cop on the Fourth of July, 1974. And unfortunately, there were others, all with similar stories of stupid self-destruction and broken-hearted families. May they all rest in peace; the same could have happened to any one of the rest of us dozens of times.

* * * *

I reflected on Lawrence, who'd left the apartment and Maryland about six months ago, not long after the band broke up. We'd been gigging pretty regularly and had recorded some quality demo tapes. But the rest of the band members always knew that Lawrence, Prince George's County's very own guitar god, was the star. When he got a sweet offer to tour the South with a much better band, he split and our band ceased to exist. The fact that Jennie had broken his heart hadn't helped the matter any.

I had been getting letters and phone calls from Lawrence on a regular basis. I shamefully admit that during my more dismal days, when I'd gotten home after a day of grueling posthole digging or humiliating roadside trash pickup with the County work crew, I used to get awfully angry and envious of him when he'd call to inform me that he'd met and gotten to play with some famous rock star at such-and-such blues bar in Macon or Baton Rouge or wherever, or he had partied in LA at the home of a rock star's wife, one of Hollywood's hottest actresses at the time. I'd be depressed for days, wallowing in self-pity over my insipid working man's life. But, truly, I was extremely proud of him and thrilled that at least one of us had managed to escape and was doing what he loved to do. And of course, I wasn't a bit surprised when nine years later, in 1984, he toured as lead guitar player for one of the top pop stars in the world. When the tour came to RFK stadium in DC, he invited my wife, Kahmeh, and me as his special guests to the show and we were able to visit backstage with the star and band. Lawrence was always a class act and he's forever in my heart.

* * * *

While waiting for Holly, my thoughts drifted to James, the third side of that ever-mutable triangle, of which Lawrence and I fashioned the other two. He had left the apartment and Maryland not long after Lawrence. As he hadn't called or written to me, my only information about him came from Lawrence, who told me that James had moved to Chicago and was working as a strip-club dancer. According to Lawrence, his *nom de guerre* was Big Tex since he dressed (undressed?) as a cowboy.

My friendship with James had never been the same since our trip to Jamaica. As I have recounted earlier*, too many hurtful things had been said and too many inappropriate and dishonorable deeds had been committed during that trip. As I sat on the stoop and recalled our actions during our Jamaican escapade, I felt the weight of something to which I had paid no

---

*   *Editor's note: Presumably in one of the missing chapters.*

heed whatsoever since as far back as Junior High: guilt. I suddenly recognized that my ganja- and cocaine-muddled memories of our time in Montego Bay and Negril, and of the curious assortment of women with whom we partied at their expense; of the two gentle Canadian gentlemen, with their classic Bentley and colonial plantation mansion, who so graciously pampered us; and of the Rastas, with their more humble, herb-centered hospitality, contained much more remorse than pleasure. I now realized that in those various Jamaican episodes, during which James and I had simply acted upon our feral Ellison Heights instincts, in one way or another, we had exploited all of those good people.

And at that moment I ceased to blame James for what I had rationalized was his toxic influence on me and fully accepted the culpability for my personal behavior prior to and during our time in Jamaica. And with a shame that I did not know I could still experience, I confessed to myself that our conning of Charlotte, the victim of my pathetic attempt to emulate James and play the scheming gigolo so that we could acquire the money for the trip was totally my plan and solely my disgraceful enterprise. And of course, unguarded, gullible Charlotte never did learn what her money actually paid for; it certainly was not for the bail to get James out of the Ellison Heights jail as she had been led to believe.

* * * *

Since Lawrence and James had moved out, two close buddies of mine had moved in. Lenny Johnson and

Woodcock, who had been the bass player for the band and preferred to be called only by his surname, were good people. They both had steady jobs and were responsible guys—a rarity back then—and since my name was on the lease, it was reassuring to know that I could always count on their share of the rent being paid on time.

However, on the negative side, they both worked loading trucks at a nearby Pepsi-Cola bottling plant and they worked the 4:00 PM to midnight shift. So, when these party-hardy brothers came home after midnight every single weeknight, often with several workmates tagging along, the drinking, weed smoking, coke-snorting, and boisterous conversations would start up and last for hours. And Jesus, the music! To think that I used to love Parliament-Funkadelic and Earth, Wind, and Fire. After months of having their music blasted at wall-shaking volumes almost every single night while I was trying to get some sleep, my love for those bands definitely waned. (By the way, the ear-splitting music's effects on our neighbors didn't matter at all; this was an Ellison Heights apartment after all, where that kind of partying or our band's deafeningly loud practice sessions were the norm and considered an inviolable right.) But due to my respect and great liking for these guys and the fact that I would have been doing the same if I were in their position, I let them party, making only the occasional request that they turn the music down just a bit.

* * * *

Holly was nineteen at the time and still living with her parents. She and I had been talking about possibly living together ever since her parents had announced that they were moving to Florida following her father's imminent retirement. Needless to say, she did not want to move in with me at Ellison Heights.

When she advised her parents that she would not be going with them as they had expected, and that she and I planned to get a place together, they, being rather conservative folk, were scandalized and extremely angry. Subsequently, her father, a US Army colonel, telephoned me and gruffly summoned me to their house.

It took me over an hour to hitchhike to their College Park home. I smoked a joint before knocking on their door. Moments later, while sitting on their plastic-covered living room sofa, surrounded by walls bursting with photographs of Holly at every possible demarcated stage of growth in her life, I was read the hackneyed but still effective riot act and was hectored with the even more egregious "you just want to get the milk without having to buy the cow" harangue. But plucky Holly stood (actually sat) firmly by her long-haired, earring-wearing, very stoned boyfriend and essentially told her parents to shove it and, yanking me by the hand, led me out of the house. I felt kind of sorry for her parents; they were decent people for whom I should have had more respect.

* * * *

Just a few weeks following our clash with her parents, with whom she had reconciled and who had very reluctantly accepted her decision, Holly blew into my apartment—of course made easier by the missing doorknob—exultant with the news that she had found a condo for us that was for rent in a much nicer part of town. Someone at her job had told her of a military couple who was being transferred to Korea and wanted to rent their condo quickly and at a reduced rent. We visited them the next day. When I walked into their upscale, shag-rugged condo I felt as if I was entering The Ritz, considering the hovel where I'd been living. We signed the lease on the spot.

I immediately let Lenny and Woodcock know of my plans, and since neither of them wanted to assume my apartment's lease, they were already moved out on that day when I made my final exit.

* * * *

As I sat on the stoop that day waiting for Holly, it started snowing lightly, a somewhat rare occurrence for the month of November in Maryland. A few minutes later I watched as she pulled up in the 1966 Mustang her parents had given her for her high school gradua-tion. My effervescent, warmhearted Maryland girl was coming to my rescue again.

Since I'd met Holly just over a year before, I had felt myself gradually changing, mellowing under her mollifying spell of tenderness and sweet promise. She was the first to begin softening my shell and resurrecting my human decency. She made me feel like I could be a McCullough boy again.

As I walked to her car, I remembered that I wanted to tell her of my telephone conversation with the Monarch in Exile the evening before. My father, who had recently married Julie, a fellow professor at George Washington University, informed me that he, Julie, and her two little boys were moving to northern California in a couple of months. He also said that on their way to California they were going to stop in Las Cruces, New Mexico, and visit for a few days with Jorge, his wife, and their two-year-old daughter. He became very weepy when he spoke about also visiting Arturo's grave in California; he had been so shaken and distraught when Arturo had been killed there in a car crash the year before. And I hadn't been very sensitive to my father's desperate need to talk about his beloved nephew during the time immediately after Arturo's death as I was stoned stupid most of the times he called.

I got in the car, kissed Holly hello, and we were off. As we drove out of the apartments' parking lot and toward our new home together, I looked back and silently bid farewell to that part of my youth during which I had so foolishly decided to challenge the rapids, cockily thinking that my illusory armor would protect me from the knife-edged rocks. Of course I slammed into many rocks, but I stayed afloat, I never capsized, and at that very extraordinary moment, with Holly at my side, I felt that I could finally admit to myself that the rocks had indeed hurt like hell.

As we drove the snow began to fall harder. I lowered my window and stuck my arm straight out with my palm upturned. Large, soft, wet snowflakes fell onto my palm. I brought my arm in and quickly licked the snowflakes off my palm.

Holly gave me a funny look and said, "What the heck are you doing, F.P.?"

"I am tasting the future, my love, again."

The End

Reading Books

Every day I chip away at the adamant marble,
The marble inherited from my dear parents.
(Gracias, Mamita y Papito, por nuestra fuerza.)
With every stepping-stone volume I read, I am
 seeking
Something singular to help me chip away at the
 marble.

Every unread book holds the potential
To provide me with an untried and sharper chisel.
(Gracias, Mamita y Papito, por nuestra fuerza.)
So on and on I venture, swallowing word after
 word after word,
Absorbing precious sustenance to help me chip
 away at the marble.

Every day I solipsistically sculpt myself,
Searching for my final form within the unfeeling
 marble.
(Gracias, Mamita y Papito, por nuestra fuerza.)
Some days I prefer to wear the mask of Phidias;
I look rather silly but it helps me to chip away at
 the marble.

Every finished book brings in its wondrous wake
Another soupçon of wisdom and some very
    pregnant apercus.
(Gracias, Mamita y Papito, por nuestra fuerza.)
But what will I discover and what will be the
    ultimate result
When I am done chipping away at the confounded
    marble?

Author's Postscript

MY FIRST ATTEMPT AT WRITING this book, almost forty years ago, was a failure.

I was extremely upset about my failure and the painful truth it revealed regarding my self-inflicted ignorance. I was deeply embarrassed by the distressing recognition that my education had practically ceased upon my departure from McCullough Academy. I guess I could say I received a sort of education after McCullough, but it certainly didn't include any book-learning, as they used to call it.

I realized I had to make significant changes in my life. And I don't mean cosmetic chameleon color-changing; such reflexive, adaptive changes came naturally to me, and I generally didn't need to consciously work at making them. What I needed at this point was a major metamorphosis. But how was I supposed to do this?

I knew without a doubt that the primary thing I needed to change was how I spoke, my vocabulary, the very way I communicated with people. I spoke in a mongrelized patois that was part DC ghetto and part southern Maryland redneck, all infused with a bogus Jamaican inflection that I imagine must have really gotten on people's nerves. And I used a lot of curse words; almost every adjective, noun, and verb I spoke was a curse word. I don't recall her exact words, but Holly once said to me as we prepared to enter an insurance agent's office something to the effect of, "Could you please watch what you say? And how you say it?" I didn't get angry with her because I knew she was right.

There were other things I needed to change: the excessive marijuana smoking and alcohol drinking, the long hair, and the provoking earring (Tennessee's marijuana leaf earring). So, the long hair and earring went first, and then over a period of months I stopped both the marijuana and alcohol consumption. I always knew I could summon the discipline to quit such habits. (I kept smoking cigarettes until I quit cold-turkey a week before my daughter was born years later.)

The language and lack of education issues still needed to be addressed. So, on New Year's Day 1977, at the age of twenty-two, I did something I'd never done before or since: I made a resolution. I resolved to get myself an education. Next I needed to figure out how.

One thing I knew for certain was that I did not want a college degree. For some inscrutable reason that I have yet to figure out, I did not want a college education. And it's not that I wasn't willing to do the intensive work or studying that college requires or that I wasn't willing to take specific college classes that pertained to my job at the time—rodman with a county survey crew—I just had an inexplicable aversion to pursuing a college education. There wasn't any particular professional career I wished to prepare for anyway. So I found myself suffering through a sort of existential paralysis caused by my not knowing what path to take to attain an education.

Then a sort miracle happened. A month or so after having made my resolution, I read an article in the *Washington Post* that furnished me with precisely what I needed at that uneasy, tentative stage of my life: a clearly signposted route by which I could access the all-embracing knowledge I so keenly sought.

The article was about a school, Whitman College in Frederick, Maryland, that offered a very unique curriculum. According to the article, Whitman's liberal arts program was based on the close reading of the most influential works of Western civilization, from the Greeks and Romans through the medieval, Renaissance, Enlightenment and Romantic periods, and all the way through the major part of the twentieth century. The core of their program was what they called the Reading List, a catalogue of all the required books according to each college year: Greeks and Romans during the freshman year, medieval and Renaissance during the sophomore years, and so forth. Oh my God, I thought, I had found my catalyst and blueprint, the method for attaining my education!

I called the school the same day and requested that a copy of the Reading List be mailed to me. A week later I had it, as I still do, as it lies before me on my desk, with all of my many penciled notes along its margins.

I felt a quiver of exhilaration as I reviewed that list, somehow intuiting that it would profoundly shape my core principles, convictions, and individual worldview. I had no clue as to who Aristophanes, Plutarch, Kierkegaard, Dubois or most of the scores of authors on the list were, but I would find out.

I had loved books as a child, but I hadn't read a book for years. And so the epiphany arrived as with a flourish of trumpets. With absolute assurance I knew exactly what I had to do: I would make my way through the list, one book at a time, on my own without having to attend Whitman College. I supposed that every single one of those books could most likely be borrowed from the public library or purchased at the University of Maryland's bookstore.

I realized that to acquire such an "education" would take years, most likely decades. I would need to be patient, persistent, methodical, and resolute. But I was confident that I could be all of those things since I had learned something about myself many years before: I was not born to be a hare.

F.P.R.

Pity the Poor Autodidact

No, silly, autodidacts are not people
Who lecture us on car engines;
They're just peculiar, petulant individuals,
Aspiring polymaths, every single last one of them,
That require no ivy-walled Oxbridge camaraderie.

It's hard to imagine, but they feel no need
For the frenzied cheering at the big Yale game;
Or for drunkenly singing banal fight songs;
Or for punting on the Cam, thank you very much;
Or for unpleasant parrying with uninspiring profs;
Or for dueling with sardonic dons;
Or for teary-eyed reminiscing about the beloved
     Alma Mater.

And of course, they have absolutely no need what-
     soever
For shrines with dusty-framed sheepskins on the
     wall.
(The Great Cham, Abe, and Harry S. didn't need
     them!)
No, my dear, please understand:
Autodidacts are just harmless, knowledge-mad
     fools
Who are more than happy to gladly
Suffer the loneliness of the long-distance scholar.

The Civil Warrior

You are steel in the soft crepuscular light;
You don the uniform, still plumed-hat proud;
You're to ride with Stuart's cavalry tonight,
To scout and outflank the clamorous crowd.

Sage generals have shaped the battle plans;
Old Marse Robert could have done no better;
Staff members grasp them in their eager hands,
Dying to fulfill them to the letter.

And you'll plead: Oh my God, lay me down!
Please just allow me to withdraw and cease;
God, please let me cross over the river
And rest under the shade of the trees.

A pugnacious public will regard each team;
Whose side shall they honor and choose?
Not in my backyard! They will howl and scream;
Again you'll be threatened with the civic noose.

So the communal combat will be fiercely fought;
Antietam will seem like a playground fight.
This is what two score years in the yoke have
    wrought;
With luck, tonight you'll be home by midnight.

And you'll plead: Oh my God, lay me down!
Please just allow me to retire and cease;
God, please let me cross over the river and
Rest under the shade of the trees.

A Letter to My Father

Querido Papi,

Primero, por favor perdoname for writing in English. I can never forget your well-intentioned edict that Jorge and I always communicate with you, and with each other, in Spanish so that we would not forget our native language. And I'd say that it has served us well as we both can reasonably get by with our passable Spanish, especially considering the states in which we currently reside—Jorge in New Mexico and I next door in Arizona.

Of course, at first, during our early years in this country, it was naturally easy for us to speak to you and Mami in Spanish. As we got older, however, and became more and more Americanized, it became more difficult for Jorge and me to abide by your edict, especially when speaking to each other. Do you remember how you used to punish us if you caught us speaking in English to each other? You would have us sit at the dining room table, each with a Spanish-language dictionary in front of us, and make us copy out page after page of words

and every single one of their definitions, sometimes for what seemed like hours.

A while back I got to thinking about the
gradual deterioration of our relationship, and,
in particular, the tragic collapse of commu-
nication between us during the last years of
your life. I realized, with the shock of a sudden
recognition as well as the self-castigation I
deserved for my obtuseness in taking so long
to figure it out, that your language edict was
a major culprit in the demise of our relationship. Whether in person or via the telephone,
our infrequent but crucial conversations were
essentially monologues on your part for the
simple reason that due to my love and respect
for you, I, a grown man in his fifth decade, yet
still complying with childlike devotion to an
archaic decree, could only speak in my inad-
equate Spanish, a language in which I could
not possibly discuss or describe my innermost
and complicated thoughts and feelings about
the issues at hand. I lacked the courage to ask
you to allow me to speak in English so that we
could properly communicate.

I am certain that you recall the letter you
wrote to me (in perfect English), several years
before your death, a letter in which you harshly
condemned me and derisively questioned
whether I was again abusing drugs or having
psychological problems or just being a rotten
son for not communicating with you more

often. I still have that heartbreaking letter, and, as you well know, I never answered it. If I had, I would have assured you that I hadn't touched an illegal substance in many years and that I was every bit as sane and rational as you, and no, I wasn't just being a rotten son. During that chapter in my life, I was experiencing serious personal difficulties of such a trying and knotty nature that I very much would have wished to discuss them with you and to listen to your sage counsel, but I couldn't adequately do so—in Spanish.

I want to let you know that I am about to finish writing a book of memoirs in which you, of course, play a major role. Indeed, in some ways I think you may be stealing the show, so to speak. In the book, I have lovingly dubbed you the Monarch in Exile because of your inveterately imperious character and dignity. With this letter I am figuratively knocking—no, banging—on your castle's door, the castle to which I have not gained entrance since early childhood, in large part due to the unbridgeable moat of language that you built and which I never had the cojónes to swim across.

And at this point, years after your death, it may be too late for all that; God only knows. With this letter I do not wish to convey even a hint of ingratitude for all that you did for Jorge and me, the sacrifices you made for us, and the invaluable things you taught us—or to imply

that our life with you was nothing but the
trial of tears and abuse that an overly sensitive reader of my memoirs may imagine. Given
the choice between a man who is an accessible
father but an indifferent mentor and a man who
is an inaccessible father but a most devoted
mentor, I'll choose the latter every time. The
father eventually leaves us, but the inestimable
gift of his wisdom never does. In other words,
Papi, I would always choose you.

During the time that I've been writing my
book, I have often wondered what its readers
will make of you, the Monarch in Exile. The
portrait I have painted of you, although unfinished as I write, has been as accurate and honest
as I could make it. It is a true reflection of the
image of you that is embedded in my mind,
with all your grandeur, your peasant rigidity,
your Iberian passion for life, and your Jesuitical
embrace of hardship. But I do not know what
readers will think of you as a person and as a
father. Perhaps I am standing too close to the
canvas.

Over the years I have told many stories
about you to those close to me, and of course,
many of them met you and got to spend some
time with you. Unfortunately, their reaction to
you, especially the response from wives and girl-
friends at the time we were together, does not
provide a very positive portent of how readers
will consider you. As a whole they did not like

you. They believed that you were cold, aloof, devoid of empathy, and pompous—an uncaring father and grandfather. With your aristocratic defenses securely in place, you did not allow them to get close to you. You even denied them the opportunity to observe the kindness and gentleness with which you treated your two young stepsons after you married Julie, a kindness and gentleness you never offered to Jorge and me but which I was able to witness on those occasions when I visited you and your new family by myself. And I didn't grow angry or envious when I watched you affectionately tussling with the boys because I was sincerely happy for you. I knew that you had achieved yet another metamorphosis, and at last you were at peace and no longer warring with life. No, the women in my life never had the opportunity to truly know you and understand you because for some inscrutable reason, you refused them entry into the castle.

And it's not that I didn't defend you and explain to them the type of man you really were, or the terrible storm and stress that you had endured, or how you were the stalwart helmsman who wisely steered our family intact through the daunting waters of emigration and assimilation in America. I did so with an apostle's passion and a son's love and by my rejection of the judgment they passed on you. And I continue to do so. As an artist who, weary of fruitless contemplation, hungers to complete a work on which he has struggled for years, I will now try to finish my portrait of you as best I can, and by doing so I hope that I may better illuminate and, in a modest sense, vindicate your proud, impermeable nature. I know I state the obvious when I say that a man of your substance does not need vindication from the likes of me; maybe in an oblique fashion I am only attempting to absolve my own deep-rooted need to think the best of you.

A long time ago, you introduced Jorge and me to a metaphor, contained in one of your many edifying discussions with us, of the protective armor that each of us gradually attains following every major emotional struggle or episode of acute suffering in our lives, like the hardening of a tortoise's shell as it ages. You explained that with each such experience our armor is fortified, as if emotional vigor were being deposited into our personal bank account of emotional resilience for use in future contests with misery—a sort of mercenary twist on Dostoyevsky's redemption through suffering. Being my father's son, I have taken that concept very much to heart and, in fact, use it as a motif in my book. For indeed, I have no doubt that through our individual tribulations we each acquired very unyielding armor, which in so many ways aided us but also impaired us, particularly in our relationships with others.

But, for me to continue serving as an advocate for your personality and defend especially the person you became during the two decades or so following Mami's death—the same time period during which the women in my life formed their negative opinions of you—I will need to essay further than simply justifying your nature by blaming the armor. And I believe that your armor was not the sole, or even the most prominent, factor affecting your personal manner.

I plead ignorance with regard to the discipline of human psychology. But, it seems to me that ignorance is often the birthplace of conjecture, and, of course, conjecture may occasionally lead to valid conclusions. Whether my conclusions, which follow, are valid is of little consequence since the journey I've taken to reach them is all that really matters.

The concept of suffering begetting emotional strength contains a cunning contradiction, what I refer to as the paradox of strength. I contend that for most people the strength and the hard-earned resilience bestowed upon us following our very first sorrow and from each subsequent episode of severe pain and suffering that we experience is an extremely positive thing. However, such strength holds the potential to do great harm to one's humanity, for during each distressing occurrence, strength, like a master burglar, will deprive most of us, especially those of us who tend to be more trusting of our strength and less leery of its more larcenous side, of the most treasured human qualities we possess. During each episode strength will sneak into the very edifice of our soul and, having again circumvented our easily distracted conscience, will stealthily rob us of another portion of the precious compassion, kindness, empathy, and affection that we can ill afford to lose and still be considered worthy and moral persons. Eventually, after experiencing enough suffering and pain, and if we do not curb the theft of our warmest human traits or discover a means by which to replenish them, we will become cold and lost, impenetrable, and most likely, obstinately proud of being so.

Papi, in light of the above and my now almost finished portrait of you, I can only hope that those who may criticize your character, based on my honest but obviously one-sided depiction in the book, will recognize that you—and I—at one point in our lives found ourselves cold and lost, and both of us were fortunate enough to find shelter in the storm, with an opportunity to replace what we, self-blinded, had allowed to be stolen. Julie and her boys came into your life and several special people, of whom Kahmeh and Yuki are paramount, came into mine. Through their love and patience, they helped us to regain the warmth of humanity that we had so insensitively left unprotected and that was appropriated by the very same strength that was both our body-guard and a thief, the strength that we believed defined us.

Con todo mi cariño,
F.P.

The Rooster of Instinct

Stoicism can be detrimental.
Forty years in contented captivity,
Without a single shackle or a chain;
And surely, no one locked the door.

Dionysus slept while Apollo ruled;
Duty was a stern but kindly warden;
Obligation was a vigilant guard;
And self-discipline, the ever-loyal mate.

And there were honest pleasures:
Amicable books and three squares,
Career attainments, some plaudits,
And that sort of rewarding thing.

Now the shabby, gray flannel suit
Has to be discarded and burned.
The rooster of instinct is crowing,
And you-know-who is awakening.

Suggested Book Discussion Questions

1) What do you think the *Caveat Lector* preface tells us about the author's attitude toward the truth as it applies to his story?

2) Should F.P. be considered a consistently reliable narrator? For example, do you believe that the Monarch in Exile was truly as grand and fabulous an individual as young F.P. thought?

3) There are certain motifs and themes that recur throughout the book such as the tortoise (armor), chameleons, Apollo and Dionysus, snowflakes, baseball, guilt (or lack thereof), strength through suffering, the truth as refracted and interpreted by memory, etc. Please discuss these and their relevance to the story.

4) F.P. is emphatic, especially in the *Intermission* segment, about being in total control of the individual choices he made throughout the book. Do you think he was? How do your thoughts on this issue correspond to the question above regarding F.P.'s reliability as a narrator?

5) F.P. states that after leaving McCullough Academy and starting his first school year at von Braun Junior High, he gravitated to the greasers "like an

abandoned Rottweiler to a pack of wolves." Why do you think that was the case?

6) How do you think poems such as "The Soirée," "The Catbird Seat," "Porfiry Petrovich Is in the House," "The Departed Need Not Wave," "Reading Books," "Pity the Poor Autodidact," and "The Rooster of Instinct" relate to F.P.'s story and its themes?

7) Do you believe that F.P. deferred writing the missing chapters (9–12) due to the reasons given by Kahmeh, or did something else happen to those chapters?

8) In his letter to his father F.P. discusses his theory of the "paradox of strength." What are your thoughts on this?

CPSIA information can be obtained at www.ICGtesting.com
Printed in the USA
BVOW04s0701210415

396956BV00003B/92/P